Return Ticket

Eigra Lewis Roberts

Gomer

To my parents for being there

Published in 2006 by
Gomer Press, Llandysul, Ceredigion SA44 4JL
www.gomer.co.uk

ISBN 1 84323 678 8
ISBN-13 9781843236788
A CIP record for this title is available from the British Library

This book is published with the financial support of the
Welsh Books Council.

Printed and bound in Wales at
Gomer Press, Llandysul, Ceredigion

The first sound I hear is laughter. Following its trail, I come to a small, warm room where a girl, her cheeks flushed with delight, is saying, 'Tell it again, Dad. Just once more.' He, as obliging as ever, retells the story. It's about this man who used to repeat the same prayer every night:

'Remember me and my wife,
Our John and his wife;
Us four, no more, Amen.'

The girl says goodnight and goes upstairs. In the tiny bedroom at the top of the stairs, everything she touches is cold and damp. Outside, the slate tips are coated with frost. Her fingers are numb as she struggles with the rubber buttons of her liberty bodice. She's troubled, but doesn't know why. Has she done something she shouldn't? She tries so hard to be good, to think of others, unlike the man who prayed only for 'us four, no more'.

Under the bedclothes, there is a warm nest waiting for her. She snuggles into it and closes her eyes. Perhaps she should apologize for not kneeling by the bed and plead forgiveness if she has offended, in any way, but all she does is ask God, as she does every night, to take care of her and Mam and Dad, Amen.

*   *   *

I'm sitting at the table in my grandmother's room, waiting for my Sunday tea. This is the largest room in the house, not counting the parlour, which is only used for funerals. I think it unfair that Grandmother has to have the best room when all she needs is one chair.

My aunt and uncle moved in before I was born, but it always seems to me as if they have only been here a few days and that they would both prefer to be somewhere else. I know where my Uncle Jack would rather be, but where could Aunt Kate go? She would probably get lost if she ventured further than the shops or the chapel. Sometimes, I think she doesn't even know where she is or what she's doing here.

Uncle Jack is telling me that this town where we live sprouted out of the rocks and is only a child compared to his home town in Mid Wales, a child forced to grow up too quickly and abused by money-grabbing capitalists. He stands at the window, scowling at the slate-tips. Aunt Kate, biting her nails, throws anxious glances towards my grandmother. She probably has no idea what he has just said but she can feel his anger. Alone at the table, I sit straight-backed, knees together, hardly daring to breathe. When he turns away from the window, there is nothing left but sadness. He takes his cup and plate and goes through to the long, narrow room at the back.

'Is the tea ready yet, Kate?'

Grandmother has to repeat the question. Aunt Kate picks up the teapot and starts to pour, but she has forgotten to put the tea in. She stares at the greyish liquid for a moment before she, too, follows my uncle to the back.

'What is it this time?' my grandmother asks.

'No tea in the teapot, Nain.'

She clicks her tongue. There will be many more journeys to and fro before we have our tea but sitting here, waiting, is something I have to do.

The grandfather clock chimes a quarter to six. Through the net curtains, I can see Uncle Jack standing outside the back door, looking up at the sky. I excuse myself, saying that I have to go to the lavatory, which is out in the yard. Perhaps Uncle Jack will point out the stars and tell me their names. But when I go past all he says is,

'The same sky but a different world.'

When I return to my grandmother's room, I can hear Aunt Kate coming downstairs, mumbling to herself. She passes through, smiling vacantly at me as if she ought to know me. Five minutes later, when she steps out into the yard, Uncle Jack has gone. It's a good ten minutes' walk to chapel and they will have finished singing the first hymn before she gets there, as they do most Sunday evenings. My mother finds this very embarrassing, but when she complains my father only smiles and says, 'Poor Kate will be late for her own funeral.'

The family has decided I'm now old enough to look after my grandmother. Tomorrow morning, Miss Hughes will want to know how many of us attended chapel Sunday evening. Noticing that I have not put my hand up she will ask, in a sharp voice, 'And what is your excuse this time, Helen

Owen?' How good it will feel to be able to say in a loud, clear voice, 'I was looking after my grandmother, Miss.' I take my responsibility very seriously, determined to do all I can for this old, blind woman who has nothing to look forward to. There is no laughter in this house, as there is at home. Even my father is a different person when he walks in here.

The room, beyond the glow of the fire, is in darkness. I can't see to read from the Bible as I intended, but how can I ask someone for whom it is always night if I may put the light on? Perhaps I could manage a few stories, like the one about the man who had to share the pig's food because he had squandered his money, but my grandmother, having won the Gee Medal for sixty years' Sunday School attendance, probably knows them all.

She tells me to put some more coal on the fire. When I say there's no need, she insists, saying that my Uncle Jack will be annoyed if we let it go out. I ask if she'd like a drink of water, dreading the long trek to the back-kitchen, but prepared to do my duty. She thanks me for asking but says that she never eats or drinks between meals. There is a long silence, broken only by the ticking of the clock. I can feel my eyes closing. I must not, dare not, go to sleep. I concentrate hard, trying to think of something to say. Then, I remember the song my father started teaching me, one that his mother used to sing to him when he was a boy, and which my mother put an end to, saying that it wasn't suitable for a girl of my age.

'Will you sing *"Yr eneth ga'dd ei gwrthod"* to me, Nain?' I ask, hesitantly.

Even as I think that perhaps I've been too forward – after all, I'm here to give, not to ask – she starts singing. Her voice sounds strange. It seems as if she is no longer my grandmother, old and blind, but the young girl sitting on the river bank, a girl who has been rejected by her family because she has done something she shouldn't. She is without a friend in the world and has no home to go to, for the door to her father's house has been locked against her.

'Dad said the door was only closed, Nain,' I say, when she pauses for breath at the end of the first verse.

'That's what he wants to believe.'

As I join in the next verse, envying the fish their freedom to live and die as they choose, I try to imagine how this girl feels. But how can I when I don't even know what she has done? It must have been something very wicked for her to have been locked out of her own home. What if my father is right and that all she had to do was knock on the door and ask for forgiveness? Why did she have to go and throw herself into the river? Was it because she was too proud and stubborn to say 'sorry'?

My grandmother sighs and says, 'Poor girl', but I can feel no pity. Soon, my father will be here to take me home. Perhaps I'll ask him, when we are alone, what the girl had done, but I won't mention the locked door.

* * *

9

I have another grandmother, who's not really my grandmother but mother to Dad's second cousin, Auntie Lizzie. They have a large, double-fronted house in a part of the town called Manod. I suppose both my grandmothers can walk, for they have to go to the toilet and upstairs to bed, but I've never seen them standing. There must be something wrong with Nain Manod's legs, for I've heard her say many times, 'I'd do it, Lizzie, but I can't with my legs.' She lives in the little parlour with the kettle on the fire and the teapot at her feet. On the mantelpiece, there are framed photographs of friends and what Nain Manod calls *perthyn*, distant relations and their families. She likes to be told in advance if one of them is coming to visit so that she can wipe his or her face with her apron and move the photo to the front row.

The only time my Auntie Lizzie sits down is when she's in chapel or travelling on the bus to visit people in hospital. She must walk miles during the week, through the large, empty front room to the kitchen and the lavatory in the back-yard, up to the shops, to chapel three times on Sunday, the prayer meeting Wednesday evening and Bible Study every Friday.

Nain Manod has a low, soft voice and unless she has her hearing aid switched on, Auntie Lizzie can't hear a word she says. It makes such a noise when it is on that no one can hear anything. Most of the time it's switched off so that the battery will last. On Sunday, she puts it on before leaving the house and I imagine people, hearing the whirring as she passes, saying, 'There goes little Miss Roberts', and reaching for their hats and coats.

Every Monday, she writes the sermon down, word for word as she remembers it, and then makes about half a dozen copies to send to people she used to know when they lived in Bangor and kept students for a living. It must take her hours, for most of the sermons seem to go on for ever. My father says it's a labour of love. Tuesdays and Thursdays are for hospital visiting and off she goes on the bus, having spent most of her pension on sweets and fruit. She also has an alarm clock in her bag, for even if she could afford to buy a watch she wouldn't be able to see the numbers. Sometimes, the alarm goes off, frightening everyone except Auntie Lizzie, who doesn't switch on until she gets to the hospital. She goes from bed to bed, sharing the contents of her bag and saying 'God bless', and then she'll walk all the way back because she's spent every penny on strangers who probably have lockers full of fruit and sweets.

Nain Manod is always saying that God broke the mould when he made Lizzie, and it's true. She never asks for anything, and the little she gets comes straight 'from above'. Once, she was given a pair of hand-me-down shoes. I laughed as I thought of God dropping them from the sky and people saying, 'It's raining shoes today', then I felt ashamed, for being good is so difficult and she manages it all the time.

But that shame was nothing compared to what I felt when I told my father that I would never forgive Auntie Lizzie.

We were all sitting in Nain Manod's little parlour one evening, except Auntie Lizzie, who was passing the tea around, when I asked please may I be excused for I needed to go to the lavatory.

'Not now, Helen. We'll be going home soon,' Mam said. She doesn't believe in making use of other people's houses.

'I can't wait 'til then,' I muttered, crossing my legs.

Mam glared at me, probably thinking it was only an excuse to go prying around.

'Go if you must,' she said. 'But come straight back.'

I hurried through the large front room, and out into the back-yard. It was then I saw the shed. The door was open. When I peeped inside I thought of the little house I had made in a corner of Dad's workshop where everything was covered with the slate dust that got up my nose and made me sneeze, and knew that I had found the perfect place for my *tŷ bach*.

I ran back into the house, having forgotten everything about my need to go. Auntie Lizzie was still on her feet, handing out the milk and sugar. When I asked her if I could borrow the shed to make a *tŷ bach* she nodded and said, 'That's nice', and smiled at me as she always does.

As we walked home, Mam said, 'That was very forward of you, Helen.'

'But she doesn't need the shed.'

'Perhaps not, but it's hers. Neither a lender or a borrower be.'

I spent days gathering all I needed and packing them into the large canvas bag that only sees light of day on our one holiday of the year. Dad came with me to the bus stop, to help carry the bag.

'Are you sure this is a good idea?' he asked.

'It's just what I wanted.'

When the bus came, he handed the conductor the bag and left saying he'd miss having me around.

'Are you leaving home, love?' the conductor asked, as he went to lift the bag onto the rack.

'Only as far as Manod.'

'I won't bother, then.'

He left it where it was and people had to clamber over it to get to their seats.

Auntie Lizzie came to the door.

'A cup of tea,' she said, before I could lug the bag over the threshold.

'I'll take this through first.'

I couldn't wait to get started.

Auntie Lizzie followed me into the yard. I was just going to tell her how kind she was in letting me borrow the shed when I opened the door and saw that it was full of coal. I stood there with tears running down my cheeks.

'I was going to make a little house here,' I said.

'Oh, dear. Why didn't you tell me?'

I refused the tea and caught the next bus back. As I dragged the bag up the steps, the same conductor said,

'Changed your mind, have you? East, West, home is best.'

'I'll never forgive Auntie Lizzie, Dad,' I said, when I saw Mam shaking her head as if to say I-told-you-so. 'She promised I could borrow the shed. You heard me asking her, didn't you?'

'I did, but she probably didn't, Helen. She'd never do anything to hurt you.'

Of course she wouldn't. All the anger left me but I still feel the shame and will never venture from Nain Manod's parlour again.

* * *

My friend Ann and I are standing under the old railway bridge waiting for Eleanor Parry. We were told to come here straight from school as she's got something to show us. Our mothers are expecting us home for tea and I'm trying to think of an excuse for being late. Whatever it is will have to be a lie and that means having to say 'I'm sorry' to God once again.

Ann says she can't be bothered to wait any longer and is going home. It's her mother's baking day on Wednesday and there will be Victoria Sandwich for tea, with butter icing and strawberry jam. She's afraid her brother will have eaten it all, for he's a greedy little pig. I tell her she can go if she'd rather stuff her face than see what Eleanor has to show, adding, 'But don't expect me to tell you what it was'. She pretends she doesn't care, but tomorrow she'll probably try to bribe me into telling.

'And where do you think you're going?'

Eleanor is here, looming between us and the light. Although she's in our class, Eleanor is, as Miss Evans Next Door puts it, well-developed. Miss Evans thinks it indecent that a ten-year-old should have breasts and has warned me to keep away from Eleanor Parry as if she had some kind of contagious disease.

'I told you to wait, didn't I?'

She is towering over Ann with her bosom, which is what my mother calls it, thrust out.

'Don't you want to see, then?'

'Of course we do,' I say, very politely.

Eleanor steps forward, lifts her skirt and pulls down her knickers. There's something between her legs, a kind of bandage, looped on to little hooks hanging from a pink suspender belt that stretches across her stomach. She unfastens one of the loops, holding it between finger and thumb. The bandage is streaked with blood.

'You've hurt yourself, Eleanor,' I cry in dismay, staring at the bright red stains.

'Don't be stupid. I've started, haven't I.'

I resent being called stupid by one who still counts on her fingers but can't resist asking, 'Started what?'

'My periods. I'm a woman now. I could have a baby if I wanted.'

'You'd have to get married first.'

Eleanor looks down her nose at me, the way Miss Hughes does when I refuse to drink my mid-morning milk.

'You'll catch a cold like that, Eleanor,' Ann says, in a whisper.

She's terrified that someone will catch us here, under the bridge, with Eleanor Parry showing her bottom. I couldn't care less, even if they told our mothers. There were so many things I wanted to know but it's too late now. Eleanor's knickers are up, her skirt down. She marches off, scowling and saying that she's not going to waste any more time on two ignorant little girls like us.

'Why did you have to say that?' I ask, as soon as the sound of Eleanor's heavy footsteps die away.

'She was just showing off. It happens to everyone, except boys.'

'What does?'

'The bleeding, once a month. Mam says it doesn't hurt. Come on, let's go home.'

I shake my head.

'But you can't stay here.'

'I can if I want to.'

'See you tomorrow then.'

Ann steps out into the sunlight and I'm left alone in the shadows. The dampness seeps through my clothes and clings to my skin. I will not let this terrible thing happen to me. I don't want to be a woman, having to wear a brassiere, and corsets on a Sunday. That didn't seem to bother Ann. I decide that I will have nothing more to do with her. She can grow breasts if she wants to but I will stay as I am for as long as I can.

*   *   *

16

Miss Hughes Standard Four must have the warmest bottom in town. She spends most of the day leaning back against the guard that surrounds the fire, lit every winter morning and supposed to be for the benefit of the whole class. Sometimes, I wish the guard would collapse and send her toppling backwards. I wouldn't want to see her hurt, but a few bruises and a burnt bottom would surely keep her away for a few days, at least.

Today, I couldn't care if she went up in flames for she's been picking on me for the last hour and even pretended not to notice that I hadn't put my hand up when she asked how many of us had been to chapel last night. Instead of dictation we have been given an extra problem and have to decide how long it takes for a train to get from A to B, given the distance and speed. I can't be bothered to work it out, so I take a quick guess and spend the rest of the time making up a little verse about Miss Hughes –

> There was once a selfish old teacher
> who stood so close to the fire
>   that she burnt her behind,
>   but why should I mind –

'I take it you've finished your work, Helen.'

She's standing right behind me. Her clothes smell as if they have just been ironed. She picks up my slate. There is nothing on it except a large 6.

'And is this your answer?'

'Yes, Miss. I worked it out in my head.'

Miss Hughes takes a chalk and draws a cross through the 6. She presses so hard that the chalk breaks.

'And who can tell Helen Owen how long the train takes to get from A to B?'

The hands shoot up. There'll be no prize for guessing who will be the chosen one. It's Megan-Williams-who-can-do-no-wrong.

'Three and a half hours, Miss.'

'Of course. I don't think any of us would choose to travel on Helen Owen's train, would we girls?'

Even Ann joins in the 'No' chorus.

'Perhaps mine broke down, Miss.'

Miss Hughes pinches the lobe of my ear between finger and thumb, gives it a sharp twist, and tells me to go and stand outside the room.

The door opens straight into Standard Three. I pretend I'm going to the lavatory although there are only a few minutes to go to playtime and we, as the older girls, are supposed to be able to hold until then as an example to the rest of the school.

I'm tempted to turn right, then right again, and head for home. There will be nothing but sympathy from my mother. After dabbing camomile lotion on my ear she'll bring me back, saying Miss Hughes has gone too far this time and that she's going to settle her, once and for all. After she's spoken her mind, she'll have to return home and I'll be left here with Miss Hughes, who believes that mothers should be kept outside the school gates.

So I turn left into the cloakroom, where there is a

18

row of white enamel hand basins with a notice above that says, 'Cleanliness is next to Godliness.' I reach for my handkerchief, one that Miss Evans Next Door gave me on my birthday, still folded and smelling of mothballs. It's trimmed with lace and far too pretty to wipe one's nose on. As I hold it under the tap and watch it becoming all limp and soggy, I know it will never be the same again. I hold the handkerchief against my ear, gasping as its coldness pricks my skin, but determined not to cry, for Miss Hughes will regard that as a sign of shame.

When the bell rings, I hear footsteps approaching. It's the one-who-can-do-no-wrong, head monitor, teacher's pet, top of the class in every subject except drawing, which doesn't count.

'Miss Hughes told you to stand outside the room,' she says.

'She didn't say which room.'

Megan Williams expected to see me red-eyed and quivering so that she could tell her best friend Elsie, who can also do no wrong and is second top of the class in all subjects that matter.

'You're to come back now.'

'I was coming anyway.'

I walk past her, head held high, chin up. Will she tell Miss Hughes that I was in the cloakroom? Yes, of course, that's the first thing she does. They are all drinking their milk, warming their hands on the bottles, their mouths puckered as they suck sedately at their straws, all except Eleanor who's blowing through her straw and making rude noises.

The crate of milk is placed near the fire every morning. We are told that milk is good for us, but not too-cold milk, which can cause cramp and stomach pains. I'd rather suffer than be forced to drink this horrible liquid, much worse even than cod liver oil, and liquid paraffin, taken to line the stomach and keep the bowels open. Sometimes I manage to sneak the bottle out under my skirt and pour the milk down the pan, but not today, for Miss Hughes has both eyes on me.

I'm not allowed out in the yard with the others. When Miss Hughes asks me do I know why I'm being kept in, I shake my head. A twisted ear lobe is surely enough punishment for neglecting to do my work.

'Shall I tell you why?' she asks.

Not waiting for an answer, she goes on to list my sins, which are laziness, lying, disobedience and insolence. The disobedience I can understand, even the lying – for I did say that I'd worked the sum out in my head – but the insolence, whatever that is, is beyond me.

She leaves for what's left of her break and a cup of tea which will, hopefully, be stone cold by now, warning me not to move from my desk. For the first time this morning I can see and feel the fire and I pity the others out in the yard. If this is what I get for being all those things I should try it more often, but first I'll have to find out what the word 'insolence' means, for that seemed to be the worst sin of all.

*   *   *

Aunt Kate is having one of her I'm-with-you days. Her eyes touch me as I enter. I've called on my way from school to ask Uncle Jack what 'insolence' means, but his chair by the fire is empty. I suppose it's no good asking Aunt Kate, even if she does know where she is and where Uncle Jack has gone, but I need to know. He's in the reading room at the library where there is a stuffed fox in a glass case. Children are not allowed in there because even the good ones cannot be trusted not to disturb the 'SILENCE' printed on the door.

'Did you want to see him?' Aunt Kate asks.

'Yes. I was going to ask him if he knows what "insolence" means.'

'It's answering back and being cheeky.'

'But I wasn't!'

It's out before I can stop myself. It wouldn't matter if it was some other day, when Aunt Kate had her mind switched off like Auntie Lizzie's hearing aid, but now she wants to know who it was that said I was.

'Miss Hughes, Standard Four.'

'Oh, that one.'

'She's always picking on me.'

'And we all know why, don't we.'

Aunt Kate has turned away from me. She's staring out of the window at the few plants, blackened by frost, and uglier even than the high grey wall that surrounds the back-yard. She's away again, to wherever it is she goes. A few moments ago, I wanted her to switch off so that I wouldn't be forced

21

to tell, but that was before she said we all know why, which I don't.

I leave without bothering to say goodbye. The journey home seems to take longer than usual and I feel as if everyone is staring at me and thinking – she's the one who Miss Hughes is always picking on and we all know why, don't we.

As I turn into the High Street, I see Megan's father standing outside his shop, the largest in town, staring at a poster pasted on the window. I try to slink past, but he must have eyes in the back of his head.

'What do you think of this, Helen?' he asks, pointing to the poster.

On it, in bold black letters, are the words:

Our Motto: Style and Quality.
All you need you'll find in here
For this season of the year;
All our goods will stand the test
For we only stock the best.
Yours will be a happy Christmas
If you shop at G. Lloyd Williams.

'Megan wrote the verse. Isn't it good?'

I have to agree that it is. What else could it be, having been written by she-who-can-do-no-wrong?

'And what did you learn at school today, Helen?'

'Nothing much.'

'Miss Hughes wouldn't be pleased to hear you say that.'

He goes on to praise Miss Hughes, saying what a true Christian she is, how she has dedicated her life to giving us, girls, the best education and that it will be our loss if we choose not to take advantage of this golden opportunity.

'We must not blame others for our own failings, Helen,' he says, in a stern voice.

I wish I could tell him how it was a few months ago, when I was the first to arrive at school every morning and the last to leave, when my desk felt as safe as my home. How I would have come second to Megan one term if my sums hadn't let me down and Mrs Edwards said not to worry, that words and figures are like oil and water, and read out a poem I'd written about the fair that comes to our town once a year.

She used to say that you need all your senses to appreciate words for they have a smell and taste of their own and should be looked at, listened to, and touched. She taught us a poem called '*Y Border Bach*'. It was about the poet's mother who had green fingers and could make everything she touched grow, as if by magic. Mrs Edwards brought some thyme and mint and lavender to school so that we could rub them between our fingers, for they were only words to us then. As she grew older, the poet's mother couldn't tend the garden as she used to and when he returned home one day after a long absence his heart was sore to see that the dandelion had taken over the little border.

When we were asked to draw pictures of the

garden, I had nothing in mine but the yellow weeds with the strange smell. There are plenty of them in our town, pushing their way between stones and slates, and we have been told not to touch them because they make you pee in bed.

'Don't be sad, Helen,' Mrs Edwards said. 'That garden gave her years of enjoyment and she must have been very proud of it.'

So I tried to rub some of the dandelions out and replace them with flowers and herbs, but their outlines could still be seen.

How I wish I could tell Mr Williams how it was then, but it wouldn't make any difference for he knows what they all know, except me. Whatever it is must be my fault. Is it because Miss Hughes, being a true Christian, has seen through my pretence of Sunday-evening-sickness? Does she know how many times I've poured my milk down the pan and that I spend the time when I'm supposed to be working out problems making up nasty rhymes about her? Can she read my mind, like some kind of God's spy on earth?

I leave Mr Williams bursting with pride in his daughter, who has never been called deceitful or disobedient or insolent. That's it, then, I'll be down on my knees in sackcloth and ashes tonight.

*　　*　　*

I've decided to forgive Ann. It gives me a warm feeling inside, which is something I need after all

24

that shivering last night. It was probably a complete waste of time, for I don't intend drinking my milk if there's any chance of smuggling it out, and the first thing I did when I got into bed was finish the poem about Miss Hughes:

There was once a selfish old teacher
who stood so close to the fire
   that she burnt her behind,
   but why should I mind
because I, for one, wouldn't miss her.

Ann's brother comes to the door. He's getting to look more like a pig every day. When I ask him to tell Ann I'm here, he grunts. I push past him into the kitchen. Mrs Pugh, in her flowered cross-over apron, is preparing the Sunday roast so as to be able to concentrate on the service tomorrow morning.

'Oh, it's you, Helen,' she says.

Mrs Pugh doesn't like people calling at her house, for they disturb her routine.

'Ann's gone. She was going to call for Megan. Perhaps you'll catch them if you hurry.'

I leave her to her roast and her disgusting little Porky Pugh who's picking at something from a bowl, but I have no intention of hurrying. I would rather be alone for ever more than share a bench with Ann and Megan Williams.

I'm loitering outside the Emporium. A couple walk past. The girl is a second cousin of mine and used to be pleasant enough before she started going out with boys. This one is the latest and he's no oil painting, although he obviously thinks he is.

'Ken and me are going to the pictures, Helen,' she says.

She's only stopped to speak to me because she's got him with her. I stayed the night at her house once and she showed me what she called her bottom drawer of table cloths, pillow cases and towels with 'his' and 'hers' embroidered on them.

'And where are you going all alone on a Saturday night?' he asks.

He's got shifty eyes and eyebrows that meet, which mean deceit.

'The Temperance Meeting.'

'Aren't you a good little girl.'

Brenda tugs at his arm, saying that all the double seats will have gone if they don't hurry.

'See you soon,' he calls, over his shoulder.

Not if I see him first. But perhaps Brenda will marry this one, for her bottom drawer must be full by now. Then shifty eyes will be my second cousin-in-law and I'll be invited to their house for tea so that she can show off.

Outside the Meirion Hotel, there are crates piled against the wall full of dark evil-smelling bottles emptied during the week by those who have sold their souls to the devil. In our town, inns and chapels grow side by side like nettles and dock leaves. Next door but one to the Meirion, with Woolworth's in between, stands Jerusalem chapel, solid and independent behind iron railings. The light above the path leading to the vestry is still on, which means they haven't yet started for it's turned off during the meeting to save expense.

I'm half-way down when the light disappears and I can hear Miss Evans thumping on the piano as she leads them into '*Dŵr, dŵr, dŵr*'. Any more of this and I'll be known as the second Aunt Kate of the family. It's all Ann's fault for turning her back on me. As I slide onto the nearest bench and bow my head out of respect, I can see her sitting in the front row. She's got her best coat on, for the benefit of Megan Williams, no doubt. It's not until I get up that I realize I'm standing next to Hannah-praise-the-Lord. She stinks of cat pee and her skirt is covered in hairs. Her eyes are tightly closed, her head thrown back, as she sings of the water given by God himself to all who thirst.

When Hannah has said her 'Amen-praise-the-Lord' and the echo of the last few notes played with such feeling by Miss Evans have died away, the Reverend Griffiths steps forward. Although he's only a young man, his dark hair has streaks of white in it from worrying about the state of the world and the dangers that face us as God-fearing citizens.

He holds up five cards. On each card, there's a letter spelling out the name of the devil, who is the enemy of God and man. He takes away the letter D, leaving the word 'evil', which is the result of the enemy's victory. The D is returned and the L and V put aside and we are left with 'die', something that comes to us all and which we should prepare for by rejecting all evils. By doing this we can all – and now he takes up four cards and spells out the word – 'live'.

He then asks, as he does every Saturday night, if there is anyone present who would like to share their experiences and testify to the power of God, which is the cue Hannah has been waiting for. She gets to her feet with great difficulty for she has what my mother calls 'phlebitis', which has nothing to do with fleas, although her house must be swarming with them.

We mouth the words with her as she tells how she was a slave to the demon drink and neglected her poor little ones. Tears come to her eyes as she describes how they went scrounging in bins and the neighbours threw anything that came to hand at them. We all know, except the Reverend Griffiths, who's new to the town, that she's talking about her cats, but no one will tell him for he seems to enjoy sad stories, and the sadder the better. Then one night, as she was staggering home from the Queen's Arms, she saw a light in the sky which blinded her so that she tripped over the pavement. She still bears the scars and would show them to us were it not indecent for a woman to lift up her skirt in the house of God. Any moment now she'll be into '*Daeth Iesu i'm calon i fyw*'.

I clear my throat ready for the three verses and chorus. Miss Evans doesn't bother with the piano, for she has no belief in conversions and insists that a leopard never changes its spots. Hannah's voice is loud and deep. You can hear it rumbling in her belly and flapping against her insides like the waves of the sea. We all join in, singing of how we returned from the wide road that leads to destruction when Jesus came to live in our hearts.

Before she can lead us into the chorus for the third time, the Reverend Griffiths nods to Mr Roberts the caretaker. Hannah only just manages to flop back on the bench as the lights go out. This is not to save expense, but a sign that Maggie Pritchard is on her way. She comes in from the back-vestry where she's been waiting all this time, for it wouldn't do for the star turn to mingle with the audience. There is silence, except for Hannah huffing and puffing as the result of too much talking and singing.

Maggie Pritchard is carrying a lantern with a candle lit inside. She's dressed like a man, in an old tattered coat tied around the middle with a piece of string, trousers, hobnailed boots and, most important of all, a black beard. She's singing as she clatters onto the platform of the hundred and one sheep safe in the fold and the one that wandered away into the mountains. We are with her every step of the way as she searches for the lost sheep under the table and behind the piano. Where will she find it this time? It's there in the corner where the Sunday School books are kept, but tonight they become rocks which she has to clamber over. She slips, teeters on the edge, then steadies herself. Sighs of relief are let loose here and there and melt into the air like bubbles from a clay pipe. She lifts the sheep on her shoulders, straining under its weight. I, too, can feel my muscles tightening. There it is, shivering from cold and hunger but safe and sound, as always. And we all rejoice with Maggie Pritchard as, tired but triumphant, she returns the lost sheep to the fold, where it belongs.

The Reverend calls, 'Lights, please, Mr Roberts', and we're back in the vestry. Hannah tries to get up but falls back on the bench.

'Give us a hand, love.'

She grasps my fingers. Now I'll be stinking of cat pee for days, for everyone knows that it's the hardest thing to get rid of. Ann and Megan Williams pass by with their noses in the air. I pull with all my might, but as I try to keep my balance I tread on Hannah's foot. She screams and the Reverend comes running, always at hand when tragedy strikes. As I make my escape I can hear him saying,

'Lean on the Lord's arm, Mrs Smith.'

*　　*　　*

I'm on my way to the Band of Hope when I hear someone calling my name. Eleanor emerges from the shadows behind Dwyryd Terrace.

'What were you doing there, Eleanor?' I ask.

'Snogging with Billy Jones.'

I can't think of anything more disgusting. Billy Jones, who's in his first year at the Central, has got thick, rubbery lips and his mouth is always hanging open so that the boys keep asking him, 'Caught any more flies today, Billy?' I've never been and never will be kissed like that, for you can catch a baby by kissing on the lips or sitting on a lavatory seat.

Eleanor wants to know where I'm going.

'Band of Hope. It's Magic Lantern tonight.'

'Do you have to pay?'

''Course not.' To think she had the cheek to call me stupid.

'I'll come with you, then.'

The Reverend Lloyd Davies will have a fit when he sees Eleanor. According to him and the '*Rhodd Mam*', which we have to learn off by heart, there are only two kinds of children – the good and the bad – and Eleanor Parry, who pulls down her knickers and snogs with Billy Jones can hardly be called good. But he doesn't know what she gets up to under bridges and in dark alleys and perhaps he'll see her as the lost sheep and myself as the good shepherd, returning her to the fold. I cross my fingers as we walk on towards the chapel.

As we pass the school she tells me what I said about the train was very funny and that, if Megan had said it, Miss Hughes would have thought it clever. When I say, 'Megan Williams's train wouldn't dare break down', she laughs. I begin to think that Eleanor isn't so bad after all. Maybe she's been forced to grow up too quickly, like the town.

She's still laughing when we reach the vestry and the Reverend, all in black except for a small patch of white dog collar under his double chin, whispers,

'Do remember where you are, girls.' He's too busy sorting out his slides to notice Eleanor pushing past me and settling herself next to Robert John who was caught throwing stones at the vicar's cat and shouting, 'Take that, you bugger!'

Relieved that the Reverend Lloyd Davies hasn't yet seen Eleanor, I decide to ask him if he needs any help. He's getting very red in the face and breathing heavily. He says that's kind of me and will I be so good as to put out the light.

When I return to my seat, I can see that Eleanor has moved closer to Robert John. What if she forgets where she is and starts kissing him, thinking she's back behind Dwyryd Terrace with catch-a-fly Billy?

What will it be this time, Religious Paintings or Journey through the Holy Land? It's the Holy Land with its title upside down on the screen. Robert John is up and trying to stand on his head so that he can read the words. Eleanor tickles him. As he falls over, he catches Edwin *babi Mam* with his boot and he, of course, starts blubbering.

'Pay attention, please, children. Who can tell me what this next picture is?'

'A parachute coming down from the sky,' shouts Robert John.

The Reverend Lloyd Davies quickly adjusts the slide and tells us that it was from a boat like this one that Jesus's disciples used to cast their nets for fish. Edwin cries louder, saying that he's hungry and wants his mother. Eleanor takes him on her knee and he pushes his nose between her breasts. Robert John

32

sniggers and whispers something in her ear. This is going to be a very long journey indeed.

*   *   *

All the school has gathered in Standard Three, which has been cleared for the Christmas prize-giving. The prize winners from every class are seated on chairs in the front, the rest on low wooden benches. Because I was late arriving, having been forced by Miss Hughes to drink my milk to the last drop, I have to sit on a window sill with Eleanor, who would rather be there so that she can see over the wall to the boys' yard next door. Draughts trickle down my back.

There are no paper chains here as there are at home, for they would have to be put up with drawing pins which damage the walls, but we have a tree, donated by Mr Humphries, who's giving out the prizes, and grown on his estate down in the valley. He's short and fat and, perched on a high chair with his little legs dangling, he looks like Humpty Dumpty. The tree has been decorated by the two monitors of the week, and every other week, everything bought at discount price at G. Lloyd Williams, where they only stock the best. Right on top, instead of an angel or a star, there's a plastic doll dressed as a fairy queen. I'm sure Miss Hughes and Miss Lloyd would have put Megan Williams there if they could, with a halo around her head.

Mrs Edwards reads a poem about the three kings who travelled from the East, only there were four of

33

them when they started out. The fourth gave the jewel intended for the baby Jesus to pay for the release of a slave girl who had been badly treated by her master, and had to return because he had no gift to offer. I can feel the tears pricking behind my eyelids – but I mustn't cry, or they will all think it's because I haven't managed to win a prize yet again.

Miss Lloyd, who has no time for poetry, can hardly wait for Mrs Edwards to finish so that she can welcome the honourable guest and tell us how privileged we are that a gentleman of his standing takes an interest in our humble school. She calls on him to address us and we all clap, except Eleanor who's too busy peeping out through the window. He wriggles from the chair and drops on his feet, all in one piece.

I've heard it all before, in chapel and in school and from Megan Williams's father: how grateful we should be for the blessings that are showered upon us. I switch off, like my Aunt Kate, and think back to the time when I was in this class and Mrs Edwards told me, when everyone else had gone home and I was helping her to tidy the books, that I had a special talent and made me promise to make good use of it.

When I get home this afternoon I'm going to write a poem, a proper one this time, and even better than the one about the fair. I will show it to Mrs Edwards to prove that I haven't buried my talent or let it get rusty.

The prizes are now being handed out, the little ones first, future Megans and Elsies, if that's possible. When it's their turn they both stand while Miss Lloyd tells our guest how they have come top of every class since their very first term. Beside me, Eleanor makes a disgusting noise in her throat as if she's going to throw up, but quickly turns it into a cough when Miss Hughes glares at us.

Mr Humphries is thanked once again, this time for his most beneficial address, and we all file back to our different classrooms. Only Megan and Elsie remain, for they have been invited to share the tea and biscuits with the teachers and the honourable guest. The door is left open between us and Standard Three so that they can keep an eye on us, but there's no need for we are quite content to sit quietly watching the dancing flames and feeling their warmth.

Ann is waiting for me by the gate.

'Would you like to come to my house for tea?' she mumbles, head down, too ashamed to look me in the face.

I tell her that I'm going to my grandmother's for tea for I don't fancy sitting at a table with piggy Pugh and Mrs Pugh, upset at having to break her routine, and especially with one who wore her best coat for the benefit of Megan Williams and turned up her nose at me.

Aunt Kate has gone to a meeting in chapel to arrange the Christmas party. She must have had another of her I'm-with-you days. So it's only Uncle Jack and grandmother, both in separate rooms with nothing to say to one another.

'No prize again today, Uncle Jack.'

'The same ones, was it?'

'Yes, the same ones. Mr Humphries, Plas, gave out the prizes.'

'Mr Moneybags himself! Bloody little capitalist.'

'He looked more like Humpty Dumpty.'

It's so good to hear him laugh. I'm glad Aunt Kate isn't here so that I can enjoy hearing him swear and join in the laughter. I decide that the poem I'm going to write will be about Uncle Jack, how hard he tries to make things grow in this shallow soil, how angry he is sometimes and how sad, most of the time, because he'd so much rather be back in his Montgomeryshire, where the land was green and soft.

I can hear my grandmother calling, 'Is that you, Helen?'

There will be no more laughter here today.

'You'd better go to her, Helen,' Uncle Jack says, with a sigh.

'It's time I went home.'

'Just a few minutes.'

Because he would probably get the blame if I left without seeing her, I do as my Uncle Jack tells me. As I go through into the room where it is always night, I'm thinking that even if I manage to write the poem I won't be able to show it to Mrs Edwards or my parents, for it would be like giving away a secret. Perhaps I'll write about Christmas instead, so that they can all share it.

*   *   *

36

Where we live is not a terrace or a street. It has a private road and comes to a dead end, which means no one comes here except for a purpose. When I called it 'our street' once, Miss Evans got very upset and said it was time I realized how lucky I am to be living in a part of town that attracts the better class of people. Between numbers one and ten there are three old maids, five couples, Edwin *babi mam* and his parents, and Mam and Dad and me, of course. There's no going in and out of houses to beg and borrow, no leaning on gates, gossiping and making mountains out of molehills. Front and back doors are closed and have to be knocked on, only when necessary. We have Methodists, Wesleyans, Independents and Baptists, and Mrs Lewis, who's Church, and not one of them would ever consider selling his or her soul to the devil for all the tea in China.

Miss Jones, Number Three, next door on the other side, is a member of another Methodist chapel, and what Mam calls a good neighbour. She's very quiet and reserved, never complains, and is welcome in all the shops. After every meal, she comes out with her little teapot and empties it in the garden, for she believes tea leaves help the flowers to grow, which they don't. Number seven has a small window in the door so that Edwin's mother can check who's there and whether they look fit enough to enter. Once, when he had the flu, Edwin's father was sent to stay with his sister. He was a different man when he returned, having been looked after and given every comfort, but it didn't last long. I'm sure

Edwin's mother would not have missed him if he had stayed away for ever.

There are three houses between our road and the main street and you have to be on the look-out when passing the middle one. I used to think Mrs James who lives there was a witch, but when I told my father that I was afraid she'd put a curse on me, he said she was only a harmless old woman who just wanted to be left alone.

'Doesn't she like us?' I asked.

'I don't think she does. People have been very unkind to her in the past.'

But that doesn't give her the right to come out with a bucketful of soapy water and throw it over our feet. Dad says the water is meant to clean the gutters and that all we have to do is walk on the other side, which is what I usually do, unless I forget. I did that last week, and because I couldn't cope with sums as well as cold, wet feet, I spent the morning writing a verse about the harmless old woman who takes her revenge on us:

> Mrs J is as mad as a hatter,
> not a witch, but what does that matter
>> when you cannot get past
>> without getting a blast
> of water that's meant for the gutter.

Three of the houses belong to Miss Evans, having been built by her great-grandfather and left to her. My mother is always saying that we must not cross her in any way for we can only just manage the rent as it is. Miss Evans is touchy and easily hurt, so I have to be very careful. When I can't trust myself to speak I nod and then she'll ask, 'Haven't you got anything to say for yourself?' If I do speak, she'll say, 'Little children should be seen and not heard' or 'Empty vessels make most noise'. So I try to keep out of her way as much as possible. I won't be able to do that next year, for she teaches Scripture at the County School, and that's where I'll be if I pass the Scholarship.

Miss Evans is a great believer in plain speaking – as long as she's the one doing it. But there are others who hold the same belief and do not have to turn the other cheek because of the rent, and they give as good as they get. I've stopped counting the shops in which she will not set foot ever again, people she will never look at, let alone speak to. The list is getting longer every month, and there will be many more now that it's nearly Christmas. Miss Evans will be called upon to play the piano at parties and socials and concerts, which she will regard as taking advantage of one who cannot refuse. If she's not called upon, there will be questions asked and some of them answered, leading to much plain speaking. My mother will be summoned next door and obliged to listen in silence to the usual 'The more one does, the less respect one gets'. She'll return to tell my father what she would have liked to have said, if only.

Last Christmas, Miss Evans said there would be no more piano playing and my mother lived in hope for a few weeks. A year later, she's still thumping the keys and Mam is still suffering from having to bite her tongue. There will be another summons soon when she hears that the Reverend Lloyd Davies has asked Mrs Rees, The Emporium, to play at the concert, and no wonder, for he knows exactly what Miss Evans thinks of him. So it'll be threats to end it all once again and my mother will cross her fingers and hope in vain.

It's only the third day of the Christmas holidays and I must think of something to do or else I'll be tempted to call for Ann. I know now why she asked me to tea. Megan Williams has dumped her and is strutting around town with Elsie, her close second. She had her picture taken for the local paper and wants nothing more to do with one like Ann, who'll be lucky if she gets into the A form.

I take my racquet and ball and go outside. The slate tips are sprinkled with snow as if someone has spilt talcum powder all over them. This is where I practised last summer when I was hoping to join the tennis club, counting how many times I could hit the ball against the garden wall.

I've just reached twenty, which is a record, and in my excitement I strike the ball with all my might. It goes flying over Miss Evans's wall and in through her parlour window. The sound of breaking glass brings her running to the door, purple-faced and breathing fire.

'Who-did-this?' she shouts, with finger space

between the words, a silly question for there's no one else around.

'Me, Miss Evans.'

'You wicked, wicked girl.'

'I was playing tennis.'

'In the middle of winter? What a stupid thing to do!'

She reaches for her father's stick – which hangs on the hat stand so that if any strangers happen to call they will think there's a man in the house – then leans over the boundary wall, and raps on our door. When my mother appears, her only concern is for me, thinking that I've hurt myself. Miss Evans soon puts her right, however, saying that parents these days have no control over their offspring and to spare the rod is to spoil the child. I try to explain that it was an accident but I can't get a word in.

'Have you apologized, Helen?' my mother asks, in a small, tight voice.

'No, she hasn't.'

'I'm sorry, Miss Evans,' I mumble.

'Sorry won't mend my window.'

I notice that my mother is clenching her fists.

'We'll pay for the damage, of course.'

'I should think so, indeed, and there's also the rent to be discussed. Will you tell Mr Owen to call in as soon as he's had his tea?'

She's gone, banging the door behind her, which is not a very respectable thing to do. So much for 'love thy neighbour' and 'forgive us our trespasses'.

In the square across the river, the band is playing 'Away in a manger'.

'That woman would have charged Mary and Joseph for staying at the stable,' my mother says.

'And made the shepherds and the wise men pay at the door. I wish we didn't have to live in her house.'

'It may be her house, but it's our home.'

'I'm really sorry, Mam. I wasn't trying, honestly.'

'Of course not. But at least one good thing has come out of it. If the rent goes up I won't have to listen to her ever again.'

'Or bite your tongue. Perhaps you'll be able to do some plain speaking as well.'

'I nearly did that just now and I'm sorry I didn't. Never mind, let's go and listen to the band.'

She fetches her coat and we walk down our road, where the better class of people are supposed to live. A large crowd has gathered in the square, people and children from the streets and terraces, laughing and singing and full of good will. I see Ann standing alone and I push my way through the crowd towards her. Together, we return to my mother and join in singing, 'O come, all ye faithful, joyful and triumphant', for it's nearly Christmas and as my father says,

> We must take the good with the bad
> For the good when it's good is so very good
> That the bad when it's bad can't be bad!'

*   *   *

Someone has made a good job of decorating the vestry. It can't be the Reverend, for he could never get up the ladder. He's grown another chin during the last fortnight because of all the mince pies he's been eating when doing his rounds. He'll never see his feet again if he carries on like this. As it is, he can't bend down to tie his shoe laces and is always tripping over them. Miss Evans has told him, amongst other things, that his job is to feed the soul and not the body and that he should follow his Master's example by starving himself for forty days and forty nights. That was when the piano stool, given by Miss Evans in memory of her mother, collapsed under him and was beyond repair. She, of course, is as thin as a rake with no bosom to speak of and can make a meal out of a mouthful.

The trestle tables are up and covered with stiff white tablecloths that have 'Bethel M.C.' stamped on every corner. All the cups, plates and dishes have the same stamp and are usually kept behind locked doors in the small room at the back where the women are now sorting out the jellies and trifles. The sandwiches are already on the tables and have to be eaten first so as to line the stomach.

Mrs Rees, The Emporium, is at the piano, for Miss Evans has never been so insulted in all her life. A summons came for my mother last night, and she went next door determined not to suffer in silence now that the rent has gone up by half a crown a month. She was back in less than ten minutes having taken great pleasure in reminding Miss Evans that

Madame Rees, as she is known in musical circles, is an L.R.A.M.

We sit on the side benches waiting for the Reverend to give the signal. Suddenly the door is pushed wide open and Eleanor Parry barges in. The next moment she's sitting beside me. Her coat is streaked with dirt from leaning against so many walls in dark alleys and under bridges, and the beret – pulled down over her ears – makes her look common and not-all-there.

'You're not supposed to be here,' I whisper.

'I came to the Band of Hope, didn't I?'

Does she think that one visit, and a very unfortunate one, for there have been no more slides, gives her the right to share in what we deserve for regular Sunday School and Band of Hope attendance? Yes, she does, and she's here to stay.

The Reverend comes up to us. There are tell-tale crumbs all over his front.

'And who's your little friend, Helen?' he asks.

'Little' is not a word to describe Eleanor, although I suppose that now he's getting bigger all the time everyone else seems to be getting smaller. He's taking it for granted that I've invited her. He'll go through to tell the 'sisters', as he calls them, that an extra place should be laid because Helen Owen, out of the kindness of her heart, has brought along a little friend, a non-member, true, but isn't it our duty to share with the less fortunate? I'm at least saved from telling him who she is, for the door to the back room opens and Aunt Kate emerges carrying two large bowls of jelly.

'Not now, Mrs Lewis,' the Reverend shouts.

A hand appears from behind and pulls her back. Madame Rees starts playing '*Dawel Nos*', very softly. When Miss Evans plays it, the night is anything but silent and only a deaf person could sleep through, but now you can feel the peace. It doesn't last long, however, for as soon as the Reverend tells us to take our places the boys are up and away, pushing and jostling. Robert John is the first to reach the table. He settles himself opposite a Bethel M.C. plate piled high with sandwiches.

The Reverend Lloyd Davies has done his duty and my mother arrives with the extras. I can tell that she's proud of me for having entered into the spirit of Christmas, but when she finds out that the less fortunate friend is Eleanor Parry the look of pride becomes one of shame and she mutters, 'How could you, Helen', before scuttling away.

It's the worst party I've ever been to. It was bad enough seeing Eleanor – who has no right to be here – stuffing herself, without the embarrassment of being the first out in musical chairs and watching Aunt Kate licking the spoon as she dished out the trifle. The Reverend has taken it upon himself to be Father Christmas this year. He's the right shape for it, but that's all. He manages to get all the presents mixed up. Robert John is given a necklace, which he throws to the floor in disgust, and Edwin is frightened half to death when a jack-in-the-box pops up and thumps him on the nose.

'Aren't you going to open yours?' Eleanor asks.

'I always leave it until Christmas day.'

'Let's have a little peep.'

She snatches the parcel and tears at the paper.

'It's a paint box, Helen. I've always wanted one of these.'

'You have it, then.'

They are going to play 'pin the tail on the donkey'. I won't be blindfolded in the company of Robert John, for who knows what might happen. I can't go home. My father is working and my mother will have to stay here until the very end to make sure, as the Sunday School supervisor, that the Bethel M.C. property is returned to the locked cupboard.

I'm on my way to hide in the lavatory, next door to where the sisters are, when I hear a loud crash. My mother appears, very red in the face.

'Will you please take your aunt home,' she says, in a shaky voice.

Behind her, I can see pieces of the Bethel M.C. plates scattered all over the floor and angry faces glaring at Aunt Kate. Mam promises to call for me on her way home. I'm glad I've been given a chance to escape, but wish it could have happened some other way.

I take my Aunt Kate's hand and lead her through the vestry. The Reverend is calling, 'Has anyone seen the donkey's tail?'

Someone has pinned it onto his coat from behind and it swings to and fro as he trips around. Poor

Reverend Lloyd Davies being made fun of, poor Aunt Kate turning away in disgrace, and poor me having to leave empty-handed. Tonight I'll have to tell how I gave my present to Eleanor, who wasn't supposed to be there at all, and explain that I had nothing to do with her being there. My mother will accept my explanation, as always, but it won't stop her worrying because, as everyone knows, that Parry girl is a bad influence.

Aunt Kate stands in the lobby biting her nails while I search for her coat.

'I shouldn't have come,' she says.

Today, of all days, when it would have been so much easier if she had been switched off, my Aunt Kate has seen and heard it all.

'It was an accident, Auntie Kate.'

'That's not what they thought.'

No, it isn't. They would rather think that she set out deliberately to drop the plates, as Miss Evans wanted to believe that I meant to break her window. Is it because seeing the worst in other people makes them feel better?

I find my aunt's coat, help her to button it up, and we're away. It's all over for another year. I try to concentrate on the one good thing that happened, Madame Rees playing 'Dawel Nos'. Aunt Kate didn't even have that pleasure, for she was dragged back by one of the sisters to do whatever she was supposed to be doing. It's too soon to think pleasant thoughts, however. Perhaps tonight, in bed, I'll be able to hear those soft, peaceful notes and forget everything else. I cross my fingers and hope for the best.

*   *   *

I've been walking around Woolworth's for the past hour, buying Christmas presents, only I haven't bought anything yet. Trying to decide how to share three shillings between five people is even worse than working out how long it takes for a train to get from A to B. One of the girls behind the counter tells me to get a move on as they'll be closing in five minutes. Miss Roberts, the manageress, hops out of her office at the far end of the shop, a little robin redbreast with a protruding bosom and spindly legs. Her head is cocked on one side, her beady eyes darting here and there and everywhere. I can hear the girl who told me to get a move on sighing deeply and saying, 'Here she comes again'.

Miss Roberts has probably been watching me all this time and is coming to tell me that she doesn't cater for customers who do not offer custom for she is, after all, trying to run a business and please to remember that in future. As I hurry towards the door, I come face to face with my Aunt Kate, who is rummaging in a pocket for her shopping list, and I realize that the 'she who was coming again' was not Miss Roberts.

'The shop's closing now, Aunt Kate,' I whisper.

'There it is,' she says, triumphantly, handing me a crumpled piece of paper to hold while she searches

48

for her purse. I open the paper, hoping that the list is a short one. On it, printed in capital letters and underlined twice, are the words, 'Carol practice. Bethel vestry. Six o'clock, Friday'.

When I tell Aunt Kate she's got three minutes to reach the vestry and that the shopping must wait, she smiles and says, 'Never put off until tomorrow what you can do today'.

Miss Roberts, red-faced and red-bosomed, hops up to us.

'Can't you make a bit of an effort for once, Mrs Lewis?' she asks.

'I'll be there,' says Aunt Kate, and off she goes.

I wait for her outside and it's getting on for ten past when she emerges. Miss Roberts, her feathers ruffled, locks the door after her. I'll have to do my shopping in Peacocks now. When we get to the street that leads to the chapel, Aunt Kate walks on saying Uncle Jack will be wondering where she is and that she has some nice cold ham for his supper.

'It's nearly Christmas, Helen,' she says. 'We used to have such a wonderful time. We'd go up to the big house, your father and me, to sing carols and the lady would give us an apple and an orange. She gave me a sixpenny bit one Christmas and said that I could be the future Edith Wynne.'

She starts singing 'O dawel ddinas Bethlehem'. They'll be there in the vestry with their song books, preparing for the carol service, but my Aunt Kate doesn't need any practice. If only they could all hear her now, word- and tone-perfect.

49

She pauses for a moment and asks, anxiously, 'What time is it, Helen?'

I don't know, and I don't care. What does it matter if I never see the inside of Woolworth's again? All I want is for Aunt Kate to be who and where she wants to be.

As we reach my grandmother's house, she stops singing and peers into her basket. There's nothing there except a bag of broken biscuits.

'Oh, dear,' she sighs, 'I'll have to go back to the shops.'

'They'll all be closed by now, Auntie Kate.'

I decide to leave before she can ask me in, but she brushes past me and disappears into the house without even a good-bye. Aunt Kate's Christmas is over before it has even started.

* * *

There will be no looking after grandmother or a pretend sickness tonight, for my father will be joining the deacons in the *sêt fawr*. He's been waiting to take his place there for a long time but there wasn't any room. Then, two months ago, old Mr Jenkins the Co-op died. He'd been sitting there for thirty years and my mother thought it was time he retired to give someone else a chance. When she heard that he'd gone, she felt very guilty and went to offer her condolences to Mrs Jenkins and the family.

After what they called a decent interval, all the chapel members were given slips of paper on which to write the name of their choice and the votes were to be counted by the visiting preacher so that there could be no cause for complaints.

'Don't be too disappointed, Richard,' my mother said, as we walked to chapel the night of the voting. 'You know what people are like.'

I had a pain in my stomach, a real one that made me want to throw up, for I knew that if he failed to get the votes it would mean many more years of waiting. The deacons are all very healthy and, being quite well-off, have no worries about making ends meet.

I can't remember my father ever being ill. All the worrying in our house is left to my mother, but it doesn't last long for she believes in doing-something-about-it. There was nothing she could do this time, however, for it wouldn't do for people to know how much she wanted Dad to step into old Mr Jenkins's shoes. When he was young, his ambition was to become a minister of religion. He would have made a much better one than either the Reverend Lloyd Davies or the Reverend Griffiths. He would never terrify people with the threat of hell fire and the wailing and gnashing of teeth. His narrow path to righteousness would run side by side with the wide road to destruction so that it needed only one step to cross over. With no streaks of white in his hair, and no nervous twitch, he'd make everyone welcome. No door would be locked and no one turned away. But it wasn't to be, for there was no money to send him to college. Being made a deacon was the next best thing, and failing meant another shattered dream.

The journey home that evening made me think of Jesus's entry into Jerusalem. There were no palm branches being waved or strewn around, of course, but there was a feeling of excitement and triumph. People came up to shake my father's hand and Mrs Jenkins, all in black, said that her late husband could not have wished for a more worthy successor.

We had a special supper followed by tinned strawberries and cream, reserved for very-special-occasions. My father kept on saying how good people were and that he hoped he would live up to their expectations. 'Of course you will,' said my mother. 'And there's no need to feel so grateful. It's only what you deserve.'

My father will not be walking to chapel with us, for he's got to be there early to meet with the deacons in the room which no one else is allowed to enter. He's been checking his watch for the last half hour. He'd have already left if my mother hadn't said he must not appear too eager and that it wouldn't do for a deacon to be seen standing outside the chapel waiting to be let in, like a stray cat. Now she's saying he'd better go and not to stop and talk to anyone on the way. I hate to see him all serious and anxious, and if this is what being made a deacon does to a man I'd rather have seen his dream shattered.

He's on his way out when I notice the packet on the table.

'Don't forget your Polos, Dad.'

My mother frowns. She doesn't approve of eating sweets in chapel. He breaks the packet in two, slips one half into his pocket, and gives me the other. There can be no sharing during the service tonight. As the door closes behind him, I get an uneasy feeling that nothing will ever be the same again.

The feeling stays with me as I walk, step by step, with my mother towards the chapel, no longer having to keep up with father's long strides. That means I have more time to look around. Our town is not a pretty sight at the best of times. The rocks seem like animals, crouching above, waiting to pounce on us. Dark shapes emerge out of the mist, their faces hidden as they bow their heads against the wind. Some of them bid us 'good evening' as they pass, but even their voices sound strange and unfamiliar.

The smell of burning coke fills my nostrils as we enter the chapel. Mr Price, Chapel House, has been at it all day stoking the boiler. We take our places in the pew, paid for monthly. In spite of Mr Price's efforts, without father to huddle against, I might as well be sitting outside. I keep my eyes fixed on the door that leads to the deacons' room. At exactly five minutes to six it opens and the Reverend Lloyd Davies appears, followed by Mr Price, now the head deacon, and all the others. It's my father's task, being the last in line, to close the door. They pause for a moment, waiting for him, before making their way to the *sêt fawr*. I'm worried that Dad won't be able

53

to match their steps, which are very slow and precise, for he's used to moving at his own pace, but he does it perfectly. Mr Price has been given Mr Jenkins's chair with the cushion and padded back, facing the congregation. The others have their backs to us but, from where I'm sitting, I can just manage to see my father in the far corner.

The Reverend Lloyd Davies climbs into the pulpit, pauses half-way up to regain his breath, and collapses onto the seat as soon as he gets there. Before he gets to his feet we've all got our books ready, opened at hymn 188, for the numbers are on the board above the pulpit. He only manages one verse and takes advantage of the singing to have another rest so as to fill his lungs ready for praying. He may take a long time to get going, but once he's off there's no stopping him.

This, with all heads bowed and all eyes closed, is Polo time. Sipped very carefully, one can be made to last throughout the prayer. I peer through my fingers at my father. He's holding his handkerchief over his mouth, his fingers fumbling underneath. In goes the Polo, back goes the handkerchief. We sip together while the Reverend tells the Lord what he already knows and is probably sick and tired of hearing. People are starting to get restless, and there's a lot of wheezing and coughing going on, but still the Reverend continues. He's now asking the good Lord to bless all the members who can't be with us tonight. I hope he's not going to name any names. That's a very dangerous thing to do, and knowing him he's bound to leave someone out. There he goes, tempting fate once again. He forgets to mention Miss Francis who's suffering from one of her many illnesses. Her sister will be knocking at his door tomorrow morning threatening to withdraw their membership. Some people never learn.

At last, he decides that even the Lord can't cope with any more responsibility. I hold the Polo on the tip of my tongue, all in one piece. Catching my father's eye, I smile and give a little nod. He winks back at me. We've both made it. When the service is over we'll be able to walk home together, the three of us. Rocks will just be rocks, the dark, sinister shapes familiar people once again. After supper, Dad will tell one of his funny stories and maybe Mam will click her tongue and say that it doesn't become a deacon to say such things. 'They'll have to take me as I am,' he'll say. 'It's too late for me to change now.'

*   *   *

As I was walking down our road this morning on my way to school, I heard someone calling my name and turned to see Miss Evans running to catch up with me. How many times has she told me off for rushing here and there, saying that the better class of people never indulge in anything more than a brisk walk, which is good for the constitution?

'Isn't it a lovely day, Helen?' she said, a silly smile on her face.

I looked around at the mounds of dirty snow piled against the walls and the grey houses under an even greyer sky. It was, I thought, one of the most miserable, ugly mornings I had ever seen and so I said nothing. That didn't seem to bother her in the least, however, for she carried on talking non-stop until we reached the high street saying stupid things like 'Spring is in the air', when there's no sign of it, and 'God's in his heaven, all's right with the world', which it certainly isn't.

Her hair, usually pulled back into a bun, was hanging loose over her shoulders like the strands of wool my mother uses to darn my father's socks. She was also wearing her Sunday coat, trimmed with fur, and had her mother's priceless cameo pinned on the lapel. I thought maybe she was going soft in the head and had got the days mixed up, but when we parted she smiled again and wished me a good day at school.

*   *   *

Eleanor Parry is in disgrace. She was seen with Billy Jones behind Dwyryd Terrace. Miss Hughes is disgusted and we all have to agree with her.

'How do we feel, girls?'

'Disgusted, Miss Hughes.'

Eleanor is to be kept in during break until she learns to conduct herself in a decent and seemly manner, but it won't do any good for once the bell rings at the end of the afternoon she'll be free to do whatever she wants to. Megan Williams calls us all together after dinner and proposes that Eleanor should be sent to Coventry. Ann wants to know where Coventry is.

Megan gives her a disdainful look and says, 'That's settled, then.'

On the way home, I explain to Ann that sending Eleanor to Coventry means that no one is to talk to her and if anyone is caught doing so she, too, will suffer the same fate. I can see she's annoyed, for she doesn't like to be made out to be stupid – which she unfortunately is – so I start telling her how the Christmas party was ruined because of Eleanor, but she seems to know all about it.

'It was your fault for inviting her,' she says, primly.

'I did nothing of the sort. Who told you that, anyway?'

'Mrs Pritchard Next Door told Mam and she said you should be ashamed of yourself and that she'd rather you didn't call at our house any more.'

There is a terrible anger bubbling inside me. So that's why she's been coming to meet me every morning since the beginning of term. I think of what I had to suffer at that party and how I was unable to forget the pain in spite of crossing my fingers and hoping for the best. The bubble bursts and I can hear myself shouting,

'You and your mother can go to hell!'

I've only managed to frighten myself. Ann stands there, as solid as a rock, a look of triumph on her face as she says,

'You'd better be careful or you'll be sent to London too.'

She's off to give her mother the message. Mrs Pugh, forced to break her routine, will probably go straight to our house. I certainly don't want to be around to hear all my sins being listed, for I know exactly what they are and I'm fed up with having to confess to them, night after night.

I head towards my grandmother's house. With any luck, Aunt Kate will be out, making enemies of shopkeepers and customers because she's forgotten her shopping list yet again and has no idea what she wants. I'll tell Uncle Jack what I said to Ann and he, knowing what anger is, will understand and agree that it's a terrible thing to be accused unjustly.

I pause outside the Institute to listen to the women singing of their 'arrows of desire' and 'chariots of fire' and imagine them going into battle waving their knitting needles and wooden spoons.

'It's jam tarts and Jerusalem today,' a voice says.

Eleanor, the cause of all my present troubles, steps out from the shadows.

'What are you doing here?' I ask, forgetting that I'm not supposed to talk to her.

'Waiting for my Nan, if you must know. And what do you want?'

'Nothing. I was listening to the singing, that's all.'

'You've been following me, haven't you, spying on me? You thought you'd catch me at it with Billy Jones so that you could tell the others.'

'I'd never do that. And I wasn't spying on you, Eleanor, honestly.'

'But you'd like to know what I was doing with Billy, wouldn't you?'

I should say 'no I wouldn't', but I can't.

'If you meet me under the bridge tonight, perhaps I'll tell you.'

The 'no' must have got stuck in my throat like grandmother's pills when she tries to swallow them with a spoonful of jam. Uncle Jack says it's only an excuse to have a second and third spoonful and that she could manage perfectly well the first time if she tried. But why should she, when there's a promise of something better?

The meeting is over and Mrs Williams, Megan's mother, is the first out. Being the president of the W.I., she's not expected to clear up the mess. Eleanor's Nan is the next to appear, for she doesn't believe in cleaning her own house let alone anyone else's. Eleanor pushes past Mrs Williams and delves into her Nan's basket.

'See you at half past five, Helen,' she calls, as she crams a whole jam tart into her mouth, loud enough for Mrs Williams, who has gone some distance, to hear. It'll be Coventry for me tomorrow, but before that another step on the wide road to destruction and disgrace in the company of Eleanor Parry.

* * *

I didn't get to meet Eleanor after all. Instead of being under the bridge, I'm in the vestry preparing for the children's service which is held every two months to give the Reverend a break from preaching. I think he'd much rather be at home composing his sermon. He's written down what each one of us has to learn but as he hands out the papers he trips over his shoe laces and, trying to save himself from falling, drops them on the floor. The boys, led by Robert John, rush forward to help, treading all over the papers and ripping some as they fight over them. Robert John makes an aeroplane out of one and sends it flying across the room. Soon there's a whole flight of planes whizzing around. The Reverend, his face a very unhealthy colour, shouts,

'That's it, the service is cancelled! You can all go home.'

I couldn't care less about the service. It would have been a disaster anyway, with Edwin refusing to open his mouth unless his mother said the words with him; Llinos Wyn, with a nightingale's name and a crow's voice, singing out of tune, and Robert John forgetting the words and filling in with his own. What I do mind is the lost opportunity.

Having got home so early, I have to tell my mother what happened. She pities me for missing the chance to show everyone what I'm capable of, and is worried that the Reverend won't be able to take much more and will be forced to leave the ministry and become a clerk. She calls Robert John an ignorant boy. But if he's ignorant, what does that make me? Perhaps Eleanor will give me a second chance if I explain why I couldn't be there and tell her how Robert John did us all a favour by managing to get the service cancelled.

* * *

Megan's mother has wasted no time in repeating what she heard outside the Institute. A woman of her standing should have better things to do than carry tales. They are all huddled together in the yard when I arrive, with their backs to me. I pretend not to notice and walk on towards the main door. Miss Hughes is standing there, having sacrificed her five minutes' peace and quiet with her bottom to the fire, which is a very bad sign.

'And what have you got to say for yourself, Helen Owen?' she asks.

The only answer she wants to hear is 'I'm sorry, Miss Hughes', but I won't say it.

'You will, of course, apologize to Mrs Pugh.'

So this has nothing to do with my being sent to Coventry for consorting with one who did whatever it was behind Dwyryd Terrace. It's the mother of my once-best-friend who somehow found the time, in spite of her routine, to tell Miss Hughes that I had wished her and her daughter would go to hell.

'I hope you are ashamed of yourself.'

Perhaps I should be, but I'm not. And what's more, I would send Miss Hughes there with them, where there would be no guard to save her from toppling into the flames. She tells me I'm to go to Mrs Pugh's house, at once, and that she will deal with me when I return.

It's a strange feeling to be walking through the town at this time of day. As I pass Lloyd the chemist's, Edwin's mother comes scuttling out right into my path, and the brown paper bag she's carrying falls, spilling its contents on the pavement. She's been stocking up on Edwin's winter requirements – cod liver oil tablets, Vic to rub on his chest and cough mixture in case prevention is no cure. 'Oh, dear,' she sighs, picking up the medicine bottles and examining them carefully for cracks. She's very pale and tired-looking from losing so much sleep worrying about her son.

'Aren't you well, Helen?' she asks in a concerned voice. She's probably afraid of catching any germs I might have, and passing them on to Edwin. It's a wonder she doesn't go around wearing a mask and rubber gloves. I tell her I'm fine, forgetting that I'm supposed to be at school. Anyone else would have wanted to know why, but Edwin's mother doesn't care as long as I'm free of germs.

It's washing day in Mrs Pugh's house. She's in the back-yard mangling like mad so as to get her clothes on the line before everyone else. I watch Mr Pugh's woollen combinations sliding between the rollers. They take quite a time to pass through, for he's a large man and the garment covers all of him except for his head and feet.

Mrs Pugh peers at me through clouds of steam and asks,

'Shouldn't you be at school, Helen?'

'Miss Hughes sent me. I was told to apologize.'

She doesn't seem to know what I'm talking about. As Mr Pugh's combinations emerge for the second time she says, gasping as she struggles with the heavy iron handle,

'You'd better run along now.'

I take my time going back, wondering how Miss Hughes is going to deal with me. There's nothing much she can do, for girls cannot be caned – a punishment which would give her the greatest pleasure. I'm to be kept in during break and made to write, 'The tongue is an unruly evil' a hundred times, which will take me all week. Eleanor hasn't appeared today, so I have the room to myself. Miss Hughes and the others believe she's too ashamed to show her face, but her absence is probably due to stuffing herself with too many jam tarts, and serve her right.

For the rest of the afternoon I'm ignored by everyone. It's a terrible thing to be without a friend in the world. I'll grow up to be like Miss Evans, left all alone because of her unruly evil, and only able to smile and think all's right with the world when I'm starting to go soft in the head.

*   *   *

Mam and Dad and I are having our tea when we hear voices coming from Miss Evans Next Door. My father stops chewing for a moment, shakes his head and says, 'He's done it now.' I want to know who's done what, but I'm told it's none of our business.

I decide to make it my business, for I've enough on my mind without worrying about Miss Evans having a strange man in the house as well as letting her hair down and wearing her Sunday coat to school. Pretending that I'm going to meet Ann, I go out through our gate and in through number one. It's months since I've been here, for we don't go calling on neighbours without a good reason.

Mrs Morris has, of course, seen me coming and the door is opened before I get a chance to knock. She's very pleased to see me. Her husband is as deaf as a post. My father says that's a blessing. Unlike the rest of the houses, numbers one and two face downwards so that they have a good view of whatever's happening, which isn't much, but enough to keep Mrs Morris going.

It must be frustrating for her not having anyone to share her gossip with, but I'm here now, all ears, which is just what she wants. In no time at all I know everything worth knowing about the he-who-has-done-it next door. He's Edgar James, a history teacher at the County (second term), very respectable, not short of a bob or two, lodges with her cousin Jane and is Miss Evans's friend, if-you-know-what-that-means. I shake my head. Most people would have left it at that, for children are not supposed to know too much, but not Mrs Morris.

It seems that Miss Evans has set her sights on this Edgar James. She has taken to walking past cousin Jane's house and standing on the corner by the Post Office at exactly five o'clock on Tuesdays and Thursdays, which is when he goes to post his twice-weekly letter to his mother. According to Elen, her cousin Jane's daughter, who works in the greengrocers' opposite, this has been going on for a month. Yesterday, when Miss Evans left him, Elen had noticed he was very flushed and that, as we now know, was because of the invitation to tea which, being such a polite man, he couldn't refuse. This invitation, of course, is only a means to an end, one step further along the road to the altar.

'Do you mean he'll want Miss Evans to marry him?' I ask, a little confused, for only churches have altars and Miss Evans is a Methodist of the Methodists.

'Want doesn't come into it. He'll have no choice.'

In our town, having to get married can only mean one thing. I remember Emily Roberts, Ann's cousin, who was a member of our chapel, coming to our house, her eyes swollen from crying. I was sent out to play, but sat on the stairs instead, for if no one ever tells you anything the only thing to do is to find out for yourself.

I heard my mother saying, 'It's no use crying. What's done is done.'

Emily started sobbing again and, in between sighing and blowing her nose, said that she had always dreamt of walking down the aisle on her father's arm, all in white. My mother told her she'd have to make do with the registry office and a nice two-piece suit, and as soon as possible before it started to show. She also said that, with any luck, Emily could have an eight-month baby and no one need ever know. But the registry office and her parents' absence were enough to set tongues wagging. Ann and I went and stood outside the office the day Emily got married. We had bought a packet of confetti between us, but when she came out, wearing the same two-piece that she wore on Sunday, she looked so sad that there didn't seem any point in wasting it.

Mrs Morris is asking if I'd like a cup of tea, but I've been told everything I wanted to know, and more. As I leave, she says,

'I hope that Edgar James will see the light as your father did.'

*   *   *

There was a lot of whispering going on today whenever Miss Hughes turned her back. I knew it had something to do with Elsie, who comes second to Megan Williams in all-subjects-that-matter, for she had a silly smile on her face all day. I was so busy trying to hear what they were saying that I failed to finish my sums and was kept behind after school. By the time I left, they had all disappeared.

Eleanor was sitting on the wall outside her Nan's house, stuffing her mouth with digestive biscuits. She called out to me,

'That Elsie didn't invite you to her birthday party, then?'

So that's what they were whispering about. I said a little prayer in my head asking God to help me not to let on to Eleanor that I didn't know.

'Of course she did.'

'Why aren't you there, then?'

'I didn't want to go.'

'Pull the other one.'

Eleanor came up to me and grabbed my arm. The pain brought tears to my eyes. She thrust her face close to mine and, spitting crumbs at me, said that she would be my friend and sod the whole lot of them. The thought of being Eleanor's friend and being made to do disgusting things in dark corners gave me the strength to push her away and say,

'If you must know, Eleanor, I couldn't go because my grandmother is very ill.'

She probably didn't believe me but it was enough to send her lumbering back to the house, muttering,

'Please yourself. I don't know why I bothered with you, anyway.'

My knees were trembling as I walked on. Having asked God to help me, I had let him down again by telling lies and using my poor blind grandmother as an excuse. That meant at least two black marks against me, to add to all the others, and another step nearer the big fire and the wailing and gnashing of teeth.

I decided to take the long way home, which took me past Elsie's house, just to make sure, for my sin would be that much greater if there had been no cause for lying. The door was closed but there was a light on in the front room, which is called the parlour and is only used on special occasions. I peered in through the window, and there they were seated around the table with Elsie at the far end wearing a paper crown and the same silly smile on her face. Megan Williams was sitting next to her, nibbling at a sandwich and taking care not to drop any crumbs on the tablecloth, and opposite her Ann, who is supposed to be my best friend. I remembered being told in Sunday School about the lepers who were kept apart and made to wear little bells around their necks warning people to keep clear. And that's what I was, unwanted and without a friend in the world, pitied by someone like Eleanor Parry who doesn't need to wear a bell to warn people off.

Suddenly, the front door opened and Elsie's mother was standing there.

'Oh, dear,' she sighed when she saw me. 'I'm afraid you're rather late but I suppose we can find room for you somewhere.'

She led me into the house and went through into the kitchen. I could hear her saying to Elsie's father,

'I couldn't leave the poor girl out there, could I?'

They both re-appeared, carrying a small table and a chair, and I followed them into the front room. They all stopped chewing, munching, nibbling, and stared at me. The table and chair were set in a corner and Elsie's mother brought me a plate of sandwiches and a glass of lemonade. Elsie had her back towards me and that's how it stayed until the jelly and trifle were eaten, the cake cut and the presents opened. When her mother came to clear the dishes, I told her I had to go and she said, 'What a pity. You'll miss the conjuring tricks', but I could tell that she, too, was glad to see the back of me. As I passed Elsie, she turned towards me and hissed,

'Don't you *ever* do that again.'

I ran all the way home. Mam had got the tea ready, but I told her I'd already eaten in Elsie's house, although all I managed was one sandwich.

'And what were you doing there?' she asked.

'It was Elsie's birthday but I wasn't supposed to be there. Her mother caught me outside the house and made me go in.'

I wanted to tell her how horrible it all was, but the words got stuck in my throat with what was left of the sandwich. Perhaps it was my punishment for lying and that the black marks against me had been rubbed out because of what I had to suffer in Elsie's house. Thinking that made me feel better and I swilled down the rest of the sandwich with water, which is said to wash all one's sins away.

* * *

I'd been awake most of the night. Dad decided enough was enough and that he was going to fetch Doctor Jones. He was half-way down the stairs when my mother, who hadn't been near me all night, caught up with him. I could hear them arguing, with Mam asking if he wanted to give people the pleasure of raking up all that business of you-know-what and Dad saying he didn't care a damn and that he should have put a stop to this a long time ago. I heard the front door opening, Mam crying, 'I'll never forgive you for this', the door closing again and Dad's heavy footsteps coming upstairs. I called out to him but he didn't answer.

I should probably have asked God's forgiveness before going to bed, but as He'd already decided to punish me with the pain it would be a waste of time. I wasn't at all sorry, and to have lied to God would mean another black mark against me.

When I got up this morning, having pretended not to hear Mam calling me, Dad was still there. He asked me if I was feeling better, and I shook my head and held my hand against my ear. Coming through from the kitchen, Mam told me I'd have to hurry or I'd be late for school. I went and sat by the fire, my back to her.

'Perhaps she'd better stay home just for today,' my father said.

'She's going, and that's an end to it.'

'I'm not!'

I hadn't meant to shout. Answering one's parents back, even in a whisper, is a sin.

Mam went back into the kitchen and closed the door. I drew myself closer to the fire, not caring if I got red marks on my legs. Dad came and sat opposite me.

'Tell me what happened, Helen,' he said quietly.

'I've already told you,' I mumbled. 'Miss Hughes pushed me against the peg in the cloakroom.'

'And why did she do that?'

I shook my head.

'You must tell me. Did you do or say something to annoy her?'

'I only told the truth.'

'And what exactly is the truth?'

'That she's always picking on me. But I don't know why, do I.'

I still don't know, although Dad has promised me that Miss Hughes will never pick on me again. He told me it was his fault and that he was so sorry. When I asked him why and what for, he said the quarrel had been between him and Edna and that it was all sorted out now. I didn't know who he was talking about at first, and then I realized that Edna was the Miss E. Hughes who had written on my last report, 'Could do better if she put her mind to it'. When I showed the report to my mother I had all the excuses ready but all she said was, 'It's her duty to see that you do'.

Dad must have called at the school, although fathers are never seen outside the school gate, let alone inside. All the girls will have seen him and they'll be talking about me. I can't go back there without knowing why.

When I go downstairs, they are both sitting by the fire. It's four o'clock, but there's no sign of tea.

'Are you feeling better now?' Mam asks, without looking at me.

I suppose I should tell her I'm sorry, but why should I when it's not my fault.

'Why did Miss Hughes pick on me?' I ask.

Dad sighs. 'Leave it now, Helen,' he says. 'Everything's been settled.'

But it hasn't been, and I'm not going back there until it has.

*   *   *

Uncle Jack has told me all I wanted to know. He didn't want to, at first. He said it was none of his business and that it was up to my parents to tell me. Then, Aunt Kate, who was standing by the window biting her nails, said, 'We all know why, don't we', and I shouted 'I don't' and started to cry.

'It was a long time ago,' Uncle Jack said. 'Your father was living here with his mother. He took a fancy to Edna Hughes.'

'He never did,' Aunt Kate muttered. 'She wouldn't leave the poor boy alone.'

'Isn't it time Nain had her supper, Kate?' Uncle Jack asked. She stared at him as if she had no idea who Nain was.

'Supper, Kate,' he said again, and she trotted off to the kitchen.

'That's true, Helen,' he said, after she had left. 'And your grandmother encouraged her. I suppose she thought Edna Hughes was a good catch. She made quite a fuss when they got engaged.'

I couldn't believe it. My father engaged to be married to Miss Hughes, who stands between us and the fire and makes us drink warm milk? Miss Hughes, who had called me lazy and insolent, and pushed me against the peg because I told the truth?

Aunt Kate came in from the kitchen.

'Hello, Helen,' she said, as if I'd only just arrived. 'What's the time, Jack?'

Uncle Jack told her it was getting on for half past six.

'Why didn't you tell me?' she said. 'Mam will be wanting her supper.' And back she went.

'What happened?' I asked, afraid that these interruptions would cause him to change his mind and decide not to tell me any more. 'Didn't she want to marry him after all?'

'Oh, yes, she did. But your father met your mother and broke off the engagement. Edna threatened to sue him for breach of promise. That meant he'd have to go to court and everyone would get to know.'

'But they knew already. Everyone except me.'

'I suppose they did. And do you understand, now that you *do* know?'

I said I did, but I wasn't sure. Now that I've had time to think, it's all starting to make sense. Miss Hughes didn't sue my father. Uncle Jack thought that it was my grandmother who had persuaded her not to, because of the scandal, but perhaps it would have been better if she had.

In Sunday School, a few months ago, we were taking it in turns to read from the Bible. There was this verse about eating sour grapes and setting someone's teeth on edge. I remember asking Mrs Pritchard what it meant, and she said the children of Israel were being punished because of what their fathers had done. Llinos Wyn got very upset because she had eaten some of the grapes her father had bought to take to her grandmother in hospital and she was afraid her teeth would fall out. Mrs Pritchard explained it was just a way of saying people had sinned and that it had nothing to do with grapes or teeth, but Llinos Wyn cried and said she didn't want to wear false teeth and put them in water overnight in case she swallowed them.

Although I thought Llinos Wyn was being stupid, as usual, I couldn't understand why the children of Israel were made to suffer, but I can now. Miss Hughes picked on me because of what my father had done to her, as Miss Evans punished Mam and Dad by putting up the rent because I broke her window.

I can hear my father's footsteps on the stairs. He knocks on the door. I want to tell him to go away, but I can't. The Bible tells us to honour our father and mother.

It also tells us to turn the other cheek and to pray

for those who have sinned against us, but Auntie Lizzie is the only one I know who can do all that.

The bed creaks as he sits on the edge. I keep my eyes closed. He smells of soap and Erinmore tobacco.

'Is there anything you want?' he asks.

I shake my head.

'A cup of Bovril, perhaps, or some Ovaltine?'

I shake my head again. He reaches in his pocket for a packet of Polo mints, cuts it in half, and hands one half to me, but I keep my hands under the bedclothes.

'Where did you go tonight?' he asks.

'To Nain's house.'

'How was she?'

'I didn't see her. Uncle Jack told me about you and Miss Hughes. He didn't want to, but I had to know.'

'And you should have heard it from me. I've let you down, haven't I?'

I nod my head. All this shaking and nodding is making my ear ache.

'She hurt me, Dad. She called me lazy and disobedient and insolent and broke the chalk in half and all the girls laughed at me because my train had taken six hours . . . and you wanted to marry her.'

'She wanted to marry me, Helen.'

'Auntie Kate said she wouldn't leave you alone.'

'Did she now?'

'Like Miss Evans and he-who's-done-it?'

My father sighs. 'She was quite smart then, in all ways. And your grandmother was very fond of her. I was too weak to resist. But then I met your mother, and she made me strong again.'

'And opened your eyes before it was too late.'

He looks at me the way he did when I recited a whole hymn without a single mistake in chapel one Sunday morning.

'I was afraid you wouldn't understand,' he says.

'Is that why you didn't tell me?'

'Yes. And I didn't want to hurt your mother.'

So he let *me* be hurt, instead.

'I didn't know things were so bad. You should have said.'

It's my fault again. People are always finding ways of blaming someone else. I hope he won't ask me to forgive him, for I can't. If he tries to kiss me goodnight, I will turn my head away. But all he does before he leaves is whisper,

'Sleep tight.'

There will be no 'remember us three' tonight. As I open the window to get rid of the smell of tobacco, my half of the Polo mints falls on the floor and I kick it under the bed.

*　　*　　*

It's the first week of the summer holidays and I'm sitting in the parlour. Before she left to do her shopping, Mam told me not to let the fire go out, but I can't be bothered to put some more coal on. I don't care if it does go out.

After Mam left, I went up to the front bedroom. It's the largest room in the house, but no one sleeps there and the bed always feels cold and damp. There is a picture on the wall of a young woman crossing a bridge and I was going to write a story about her. I knew there was a house in the distance, but was she walking towards it or away from it? Maybe she was the girl who had been rejected by her family because she had done something she shouldn't have.

I had to know whether she looked sad or happy, but before I had a chance to find out I saw my face in the dressing table mirror. It was the ugliest thing I've ever seen. No wonder Mam had closed the curtains in the front room. She said it was because the light was bad for my eyes, but she must have been terrified someone would see me. Dad said this morning that the spots would soon clear, but what if they don't? I will have to live in the dark like my blind grandmother for the rest of my life.

There's a tap on the window and I can hear someone calling my name in a squeaky voice. It must be Ann, although it doesn't sound like her. I can't let her see me like this. 'Go away,' I shout, but the tapping starts again. I cross to the window and peer out through the chink in the curtain. I can't see much of her, but it's enough to know that she's on her way to the park to play tennis. She's all in white and her divided skirt, which Mrs Pugh makes her wear so that her knickers won't show when she bends down, has been pressed and ironed.

'I'm going to join the Club,' she says, in the same squeaky voice.

I pretend I haven't heard her. I can't afford to join the Tennis Club, even if they'd have me, although they probably would as they need the money. I don't suppose I'll ever play tennis again, for you need good eyesight and I've damaged mine by letting the light in.

She's saying something. It sounds like, 'Are you better?' but when I tell her I'm not she goes on to say that she spends every evening down at the park and that practice makes perfect. She holds up her racquet, pretends to serve, and shouts, 'Fifteen love' before crashing into the little fence that borders the garden. Dad won't be pleased, for he spent days putting up that fence.

She doesn't appear again. I hear Mam's voice and I let the curtain drop. I'm sitting by what's left of the fire when she comes into the parlour.

'What's wrong with Ann?' she asks.

'She was showing off and fell against the fence. Perhaps she hurt herself.'

'I think the bat came off worse.'

'It's a tennis racquet, Mam.'

'Not any more.'

'She was going to join the Tennis Club this afternoon.'

'Oh, dear. Can't you lend her your bat?'

'I'd rather put it on the fire.'

'It would be better if you put some coal on.'

I should feel sorry for Ann, but Mr Pugh – who's

just had promotion in the quarry – will probably buy her a new racquet so that she can practise until perfect. She must be crying her eyes out now, but they'll be fine once the tears are dried. And what about me? I'll never be the same again. Even if the spots disappear I'll be left with watery eyes and a scarred skin from scratching. How can I pity Ann when I need all the pity for myself?

*   *   *

I didn't have to stay in the dark like my poor, blind grandmother after all. The spots had disappeared and I was fit to be seen once again, although Edwin's mother didn't seem to think so. When she saw me coming, she scurried in through the gate, pushing Edwin before her.

The Pugh's door was open and I could hear Ann calling her brother a greedy little pig, which he is. This was followed by a loud squeal. Ann came storming out and banged the door behind her.

'What are you doing here?' she asked. 'I thought you were supposed to be ill.'

'I was, but I'm all right now.'

'Come on then.'

'Come on where?'

'I don't know, do I?'

'Shall we go down to the woods?'

'I'd rather go to the park.'

The park it was, for you must be very fit to cope with Ann when she's in one of her bad moods. On the way there we met Mr Pritchard, Ann's next door neighbour, puffing away at his pipe. He squinted at her through clouds of smoke.

'And who stole your porridge this morning?' he asked.

Ann scowled at him and said, 'It was bacon, Mr Pritchard.'

She did nothing but complain for a whole hour, sitting on a bench opposite the bowling green where old men spend their time, arguing and accusing one another of cheating. While she was in the back-kitchen buttering bread to make a bacon sandwich, Porky Pugh had scoffed the whole lot. When I said she should have taken it with her, she told me I had no idea what it was like to have a brother who would steal food out of your mouth. I certainly wouldn't want a brother of any kind, for having a boy in the house would ruin everything. All the boys I know have runny noses and smelly feet and are always kicking and punching anything within reach. I'd much rather have a pet monkey, but I'll never get one as Mam thinks monkeys do nothing but bite and scratch and should be left swinging from trees.

Ann had slapped little Porky as hard as she could, but I don't suppose he felt it through all those layers of fat.

'What did your mother say?' I asked.

'That she didn't have time to fry some more because of the ironing.'

It would take more than stealing and slapping to upset Mrs Pugh's routine.

Ann got up saying she could think of better things to do than sit there watching old men playing with balls.

When I asked, 'Like what?' she shrugged and said, 'I'm too hungry to be able to think now. Call for me after dinner.'

She called for me before I could call for her. Mam took one look at the pushchair parked outside the gate and asked,

'Aren't you two rather old to be playing with dolls?'

Ann, who once banged her doll's head against the wall in a fit of temper, said,

'It's a real live baby, Mrs Owen. We're taking it out for a walk.'

There are no babies in our family and I certainly didn't like the look of this one. It was big and fat and reminded me of Porky Pugh. Ann told us it was her cousin Emily's little boy, very advanced for his age according to his mother, and her pride and joy. She was very grateful when Ann offered to be his nanny for the afternoon. His name was Robert but everyone called him Bobby. Mam squatted by the pushchair, peered in and said, 'Hello, Bobby'. He started howling and Ann shouted,

'Stop it, you naughty boy, or I'll give you a smack.'

'I wouldn't do that, Ann,' Mam warned. 'You don't want to upset Emily.'

Since the Reverend refused to let her get married

in chapel, and Mam said she would have to make do with the registry office, Emily has never set foot in Bethel M.C. or any other chapel and she passes us on the street with her nose in the air.

'Did you tell her I was coming with you?' I asked.

'No, or she wouldn't have let me take him.'

'Perhaps you'd better go on your own,' Mam suggested.

Ann said that she couldn't possibly push him up the hills for he weighed a ton, and I agreed to go with her as long as we kept out of sight.

We followed the back streets until we came to the road that leads down to the woods.

'I'd rather go the park,' Ann said, but I wasn't going to give in this time.

He started howling again, kicking the pram and punching the air with clenched fists.

'Haven't you got anything for him to eat?' I asked, which was a silly question for they never have any leftovers in their house.

'Let's get him out and dump him on the grass,' she said.

It took both of us to lift him out of the pushchair. We sat on a stone and watched him pulling at the grass and stuffing it into his mouth.

'Should he be doing that?' I asked. 'What if he eats it?'

'It's his fault if he does.'

Ann closed her eyes and burped. She must have swallowed her dinner without chewing before her brother could get at it. I went and sat in the pushchair, which smelled of talcum powder and felt a bit damp. Ann had forgotten to put the brake on, and off I went down the slope. As the pushchair gathered speed, I tried to stop it with my feet, but couldn't. It toppled over the edge and I landed in some bramble bushes.

It took me some time to untangle the pram and myself. Ann stared at me and asked,

'Have you been picking blackberries?'

She didn't notice the scratches on the pram and couldn't care less about mine. Bobby had green lips and a very red face. He howled, then grunted and let out a loud fart.

'He's doing a jobby,' Ann said. 'That's it, I'll have to take him home.'

Although I'd never heard the word before, I knew what she meant when I helped her to pick him up and strap him in.

'Are you coming?' she asked.

'No, I'm not. And you'd better clean his mouth or Emily will have a fit.'

She spat on her handkerchief, rubbed his lips, wrinkled her nose and said,

'I've better things to do than look after stinking babies.'

And so did I. I sat on the grass, a distance away from where Emily's eight-month baby had done his business, and managed to forget the scratches by writing a verse:

Emily's pride and joy, who's called Bobby,
eats grass, and has just done a jobby;
   he howled like a banshee
   as he filled up his nappy
and was taken away by his nanny.

(I'm not quite sure what a banshee is, only that it howls).

*   *   *

We are off on our annual outing to Morfa Bychan. Dad has been looking forward to it for weeks. He's always telling us that he has salt water in his blood from having been brought up by the sea.

'That was a long time ago,' Mam says.

He reminds us of the time he took us to Barmouth to see the portrait of his grandfather in the boat house on the quay: 'Captain Owen, Master Mariner'.

'Mam used to say I was the spitting image of him,' he boasts.

'I couldn't see it myself,' mutters Mam, who had insisted on washing all our clothes when we got home to get rid of the fish smell.

He also reminds us, as he always does before the outing, of the mention he got in the local paper for saving a young boy from drowning and says that he's determined to teach me to swim this time. But what use will that be when we only go near the sea twice a year?

Even that is too much for Mam, who prefers having her feet on firm ground.

'I don't know why I bother,' she sighs as she spreads salmon paste on the bread for our picnic. 'They'll only taste of sand.'

Dad laughs and says that's why they are called sand-wiches.

The first thing my father does when we get on the bus is open the window, but there are so many complaints that he's forced to close it. He tells us, in a loud voice, how he used to ride down to Morfa Bychan on his bike and that he wouldn't mind doing that again for it was much healthier than being cooped up on a stuffy bus smelling of sweat and unwashed feet.

'Don't be silly, Richard,' Mam whispers. 'Perhaps you could manage to get down there but no way could you get back up these hills.'

Dad crouches in his seat for the rest of the journey, but when we reach Porthmadog the smell of the sea is enough to restore his spirits.

Another bus is needed, followed by a long walk, before we get to the beach.

'There it is!' my father shouts. 'Isn't that a sight worth seeing?'

Mam shivers. It takes her ages to settle down. We are told to hold the carrier bags high in the air and then place them very gently on the rug. Dad drops his. A shower of sand lands on the rug, which means starting all over again.

'Is there anything else you want?' Dad asks, gritting his teeth.

Mam lowers herself onto the rug in slow motion, saying, 'I didn't ask to come here.'

My father pretends not to hear. He starts pulling his trousers down. Mam reaches in one of the bags for a towel and tells him to cover himself up.

Dad wraps the towel around his middle and drops his trousers on the sand. I do the same with my clothes. We've both got our swimming costumes on.

'Why don't you come with us, Jen?' Dad asks.

'Someone must look after the bags.'

Dad was only being polite. He knows that Mam wouldn't consider dipping even her big toe in the sea, let alone the rest of her. She will sit here suffering in silence and worrying that my father, in his excitement, will let me venture too far. I certainly won't be tempted, for I, too, would rather have my feet on the ground, but as one whose great-grandfather was a master mariner I must try to hide my fear.

Although Dad does his best to keep his promise, even he, who has the patience of Job, realizes that trying to teach me to swim is a complete waste of time. I tell him I'm sorry and he says,

'Perhaps next time. You'd better go back to your mother.'

Mam has draped a towel over her shoulders to protect her from the sun. She has her eyes closed, which means she doesn't want to be disturbed. I sit alone, waiting for Dad to return from the sea, listening to gulls screeching and children screaming.

He's here at last.

'Mam's sleeping, is she?' he asks.

She opens her eyes.

'No, I'm not. I can only sleep in my own bed.'

We both avoid mentioning the swimming, Mam because she has absolutely no interest and me because I don't want to remind him of my failure. She squints up at him and says that he'd better get dressed. I suppose she thinks it indecent for a man who is now a deacon to be standing there naked apart from the very tight swimming trunks which has shrunk in the wash.

'Not now,' Dad says. 'Helen and I are going to build a sandcastle.'

'I haven't brought the bucket and spade.'

'Why not?'

'Because I'm too old to play with them.'

'No one's too old to build a sandcastle.'

He starts scooping the sand up with his hands and most of it lands on the rug. Mam is on her feet.

'That's it!' she cries. 'I'm going home.'

'But we haven't had our picnic yet, Mam.'

'You'd better have something to eat before you go,' Dad says. 'It's going to be a long wait for the bus.'

He takes Mam's place on the rug and opens one of the bags.

'Help yourself to a sand-wich, Helen,' he says, winking at me.

Mam is still standing there, looking very sorry for herself.

'And where am I supposed to sit now?' she asks.

'You're staying, then?'

Yes, she's staying, because she can't trust Dad to look after me. And anyway, we'd both starve if it wasn't for her and doesn't she deserve a share of the food she spent hours preparing? Dad moves to make room for her, leaving a damp patch on the rug. Mam, feeling the dampness on her bottom, sighs but decides that enough has been said for the time being. We munch and crunch, swallowing the little grains of sand and washing them down with warm lemonade and tea from the flask for Mam.

'I think I'll have another swim,' Dad says.

'Not on a full stomach, Richard.'

But he hasn't come to the beach to sit down. Two families are playing rounders a short distance away. One side appears to be losing. Dad strolls over and asks if they need any help. We can hear someone asking, 'Are you any good?' and Dad saying, 'Try me and see.'

'How childish can you get?' my mother mumbles, but she's all smiles when he sends the ball flying. The losing team is now winning and the others are complaining that it's unfair, for this fellow is obviously a pro. Mam winces when she hears my father being called 'this fellow' and thinks them very disrespectful as well as being poor losers.

All the members of the winning team shake his hand. He returns carrying a bucket and spade saying that they have kindly allowed us to borrow them.

'They'll think we can't afford to buy any,' Mam says.

She has never in her life borrowed anything and never will. But Dad is already filling the bucket with sand and telling me that this will be one of the finest sandcastles ever built.

Hours later, we're still building. My father and I are the labourers and Mam the foreman. People all around us are starting to pack their bags.

'What time is it?' Mam asks.

Dad looks at his wrist, but there's nothing there. He gets very upset, thinking he's lost his watch and how can he afford to buy another one, when I remember seeing him put it into one of his pockets for safe keeping. I search through the heap of clothes thrown on the beach.

'Here it is!' I shout.

'Aren't you a clever girl,' Dad says, beaming at me.

Mam grabs the watch and blows on the glass to get rid of the sand. We have half an hour to dress, pack, return the bucket and spade and walk to the bus stop.

We are nearly there when we see the bus leaving. Dad starts running and waving his arms and the bus stops.

When we get on, the driver says, 'I wish I had your energy, mate.'

Dad smiles and turns to my mother.

'I'm as fit as a fiddle, aren't I, Jen?'

'You certainly are. You'd have no trouble pedalling up those hills.'

We have arrived home, safe and sound. Supper has been eaten and tea from the teapot has swilled away the last of the grains of sand. Dad reminds us that we didn't get to put a Welsh Dragon flag on the castle.

'Never mind,' Mam says. 'It was the finest castle I ever saw.'

'And you are the best rounders player ever,' I add.

I wish I could have learnt to swim so that he would be proud of me and boast that I am, indeed, a worthy descendant of my great-grandfather, Captain Owen, Master Mariner. But this was my Dad's day and one that has proven, beyond any doubt, that he still has salt water in his blood although the Barmouth days were a long time ago.

*   *   *

After hours of arguing, that resulted in Miss Evans resigning from the Sunday School Committee, we're off to Rhyl again this year. It was the same last year and the year before; for to Miss Evans and some of the chapel members the road to Rhyl is the wide one to destruction. My mother, who's always said that she can't stand the place, couldn't resist the opportunity of opposing her, and Rhyl won by her one vote.

I've made sure that all the children know that they are here thanks to Mam, and as the bus sets off, David John, Robert John's brother, calls 'three cheers for Mrs O'. Miss Evans, who only agreed to come (although no one asked her to) because she felt it her duty to protect us from the evil influences of what she calls the Gehenna of the North, is sitting next to my mother, in what was meant to be my father's seat. She'll be more determined than ever now to make Mam suffer.

Edwin *babi Mam* is standing by the door under a notice that says 'No standing, please', his mother poised to shout 'Stop!' when his colour changes. We're late starting because we had to wait for the Reverend. He just managed to climb in before collapsing onto the double seat that had been reserved for him. He's all in black again today. Even the little speck of white has disappeared under what has remained a treble chin.

It's dinner time when we arrive. Edwin changed colour twice, both false alarms. Llinos Wyn, who had eaten a whole bag of jelly babies, gave no forewarning, and was sick all over the floor. Her father, who had bought her the jelly babies, was made to clean it up. They were meant to be shared, but she scoffed the whole lot, right under our noses, biting their heads off first. I think it's kinder to start with the feet. There's a cruel streak in Llinos Wyn, although she's always chosen to play an angel in the Christmas play.

When that commotion was over, the Reverend began to make some very strange noises. Someone shouted that he was choking, and the driver made an emergency stop which Miss Evans said could have killed us all if God hadn't been watching over us, and why He should she didn't know. The Reverend's dog collar was found and loosened but he refused to take it off. I suppose he didn't feel safe without it. Once he had started to breathe as normally as possible, we were off again on the wide road.

He's now called upon to say a few words. We'll be here all afternoon. It'll be tea and chicken paste sandwiches in Seion vestry and goodbye Rhyl until next year. He tries to get up but can't even get his bottom off the seat. I can hear Miss Evans whispering to my mother, loud enough for the Rev. to hear, that the Israelites would never have reached the land of milk and honey if he had been chosen to lead them. I certainly don't want to be led by anyone. I want to be out there in a land of candy floss and hot dogs, of one-armed bandits and dodgem cars, bumping, crashing, shouting and screaming, all those things that well-brought-up girls, especially those on a Sunday School trip, should not do.

The Reverend makes two more attempts, for it's three tries for a Welshman, but it's no good. I start making up a rhyme about him:

> The Reverend is stuck in his seat
> because he does nothing but eat.
> > If he doesn't stop
> > his belly will pop . . .

But before I can think of a word to rhyme with 'seat' and 'eat', Mr Price, Chapel House, steps forward. He holds up a large canvas bag.

'Do you know what I've got here?' he asks.

Llinos Wyn's hand shoots up.

'Our reward for good attendance, Mr Price.'

All the grown-ups smile, proudly, except Mr Price, who takes his work as caretaker, head deacon and chapel treasurer very seriously. We are called forward, one by one, to receive our reward, which is a shilling, and sixpence for the little ones. Miss Evans catches my arm as I pass, telling me to spend wisely and to remember the little black children. What would she say if she knew that I raided my missionary box this morning? Robert John's money is two pence short. Mr Williams explains that it's to go towards paying for a new lavatory chain to replace the one he broke by swinging on it, pretending to be Tarzan.

Mr Williams's bag is now empty, and the door is opened. This must be how Nick, my budgie, feels when he's let out of his cage. He'll perch on my finger for a few seconds, perfectly still, his little eyes hooded, his feathers drooping, as if unable to believe that he's been given his freedom. And then he's away, his wings outstretched, exploring, picking at the wallpaper, landing on the picture rail and looking down on us as other birds do, only they've got the whole sky to themselves. Like him, we, too, are still for a few seconds, blinded by the sun. Then someone shouts, 'Let's go', and we take off across the Marine Lake car park with wings on our feet.

We've been standing outside the Tunnel of Love for at least ten minutes. I don't want to be here, watching all those couples go in one end and out the other, grinning and giggling. One boy has his hand inside a girl's blouse. Even Eleanor Parry wouldn't be so bold. Llinos Wyn is trying to drag me towards the boats, but I tell her I have better things to do with my money. David John, who's standing nearby, says he'll go with her if she pays. As they disappear into the tunnel, David John turns round and winks at me.

Edwin is strapped into a car on the roundabout. Round and round he goes, his mother trotting by his side. When it stops, Edwin refuses to get off and they're away once more. Barbara and Betty Lewis, Dwyryd Terrace, push their way through the crowd towards me. They are wearing silly hats with 'Kiss me quick' on one and 'Be my love' on the other. That's just asking for trouble. Barbara asks what I'm doing standing here on my own, or it could be Betty, for they both look and sound the same. When I tell them I'm waiting for Llinos Wyn, who's in the Tunnel of Love with David John, they both laugh and one of them says that Llinos Wyn will never be the same again. They are still laughing as they push their way back through the crowd towards the Hall of Mirrors for a double helping of shrinking and stretching.

As one of the boats returns, I can hear someone crying. It's Llinos Wyn. The man who's in charge of the boats helps her out, saying,

'Turn the tap off, darling. It's bad for business.'

She runs up to me, with David John following, dragging his feet. I'm not going to ask her what he's done, for I don't want to know. People are staring at us and giving David John and myself black looks. When I cry, all I want is to be left alone, but Llinos Wyn is an older version of Edwin *babi Mam* and so I point her in the direction of Seion vestry where the sisters are spending the afternoon preparing our tea.

'Will you come with me, Helen?' she asks, through her tears.

I tell her I can't because I've promised to join the Lewis twins in the Hall of Mirrors, which I have no intention of doing, for two of them is more than enough.

Having got rid of her, I'm still stuck with David John, who's saying he'd go home this minute if he knew the way. I suggest that we go on the Figure Eight instead, for to be frightened to death is the best way of forgetting one's troubles.

It's when we're getting to where we can catch the wisps of clouds as they pass, that he says he did nothing but kiss her, which wasn't a real kiss at all, but only a little peck . . . like this. His lips brush against my cheek, soft and warm like my budgie's feathers.

'Is that all?' I ask, thinking that was certainly nothing to cry about.

'Cross my heart and hope to die.'

'Perhaps she was afraid of the dark.'

David John stretches his arms up as if to reach for the sun and shouts,

'I'm not afraid of nothing.'

Then, as we swoop down an incline which is only a promise of worse to come, he's thrown forward. He clutches wildly at the handrail and doesn't let go until we're back on earth. When we get off, his face is a strange colour, like the gravestones when my father has rubbed them down with pumice stone.

'I won't tell,' I say, as we make our way towards Seion vestry.

'Tell what?' he mutters.

'You know.'

Oh, yes, he knows. I may have promised not to tell, but I won't let him forget this. Whenever he gets too big for his boots, the two words 'Figure Eight' will be enough to settle him.

This will probably be the last time Llinos Wyn will see Rhyl. Her mother, who was in a foul mood having cut her finger slicing bread for sandwiches, gave her a sermon which lasted nearly as long as the Reverend's on how nice well-brought-up girls keep themselves to themselves and always choose to stay in the light. When Miss Evans insisted on knowing what the Tunnel of Love was, the Lewis twins told her it was for kissing and cuddling and things that could not be done in the light of day, which is true, but better left unsaid. It was probably done deliberately so as to get their own back for having to

kneel before Llinos Wyn last Christmas with tea-
towels on their heads, and not being allowed to say a
word because they were filled with fear in the
presence of an angel of the Lord.

Miss Evans, flushed with excitement at being
proven right, said that she had done her best to warn
us of the evils that lurked within the Gehenna of the
North. All those who had voted for Rhyl glared at
Llinos Wyn's mother, blaming her for Miss Evans's 'I
told you so', which they will never be allowed to
forget.

She's still at it. My mother, who has suffered in
silence all day, pretends to be asleep, but when Miss
Evans says in a voice that carries, 'If it wasn't for
your casting vote, Mrs Owen', she makes a low
moaning sound, as if she's crying inside.

Some of the boys are kneeling on the back seat,
making faces at the cars behind. They try to get
David John to join in, but he moves away from them
and asks me do I mind if he comes to sit with me.

The Reverend, who managed to reach Seion vestry
in time to get rid of all the left-over salmon paste
sandwiches and *bara brith*, for to waste not is to
want not, finds it even more difficult to fit into the
double seat.

> If he doesn't stop
> his belly will pop . . .
> and one day he'll explode in the street.

I feel quite pleased with myself. I've managed to finish my verse, the three pence left in my pocket will be put back in the missionary box so that the little black children will not suffer, and David John has left his friends to be with me.

Edwin's mother is holding a brown paper bag under his nose, but she probably needs it more than he does after all that trotting around in circles. Llinos Wyn, who's been forced to sit with her mother, has made herself ugly through crying and Mrs Wyn-Rowlands, her finger wrapped in a handkerchief spotted with blood, looks very sorry for herself. The Lewis twins, who have exchanged hats but look just the same under them, start singing 'She'll be coming round the mountain', and those of us who have cause to sing join in. David John reaches for my hand and his fingers curl around mine. One day I'll ask him to show me again what he did to Llinos Wyn in the Tunnel of Love, for now I know I have the power to make him do anything I want. I may have him as my boyfriend, but there will be no kissing on the lips and no going into dark alleys or under bridges, for well-brought-up girls choose to stay in the light even if they don't always have to keep themselves to themselves.

*   *   *

My Uncle Bob and Auntie Annie, who are caretakers of the Welsh chapel in Anfield, Liverpool, have arranged for us to stay with Mrs Pearson over the road, as we did last year. It's hard to believe that Uncle Bob is my father's brother. He's tall and thin, and droops as if he's been left in the dark for a very long time. Auntie Annie is always shooing him here and there with her do this, do that, and off he goes to do whatever she asks of him.

We didn't care much for Mrs Pearson or her house but, as my father says, beggars can't be choosers. As she doesn't know a single word of Welsh, and her Scouse is double-Dutch to us, we have to communicate by sign language. After we left last year, she complained to Uncle Bob of the rules we had broken, but as we had no idea what they were we couldn't be expected to keep them.

This time she has written them down and presents us with a copy as soon as we step inside. My mother is annoyed and threatens to leave immediately, but my father says that although he doesn't care about treading on Mrs Pearson's toes we have to be careful of Auntie Annie, who has very tender toes indeed. And so we stay and keep out of her way as much as possible.

We're out of the house as soon as we finish our breakfast, which is swallowed without chewing. As we walk towards the tram stop my mother calls in the chemist for some indigestion tablets saying what a terrible thing it is that we have to suffer like this on our only holiday of the year. All the way down to Pier Head, she does nothing but complain, of the bumping and rattling, her upset stomach, and the strain of having to bite her tongue as she is forced to do every day of her life because of 'her next door'.

She's still at it as we board the ferry. My father reaches in his pocket for a packet of Polo mints and says,

'Let's see who can make one last until we get to New Brighton. An ice cream for the winner.'

I don't expect Mam to join in, and it's quite a shock to see her reaching out for one of the mints. Dad smiles and tells her that she hasn't a hope of beating two experts like us. For the rest of the journey, we concentrate on sipping, but before we get to the landing stage I can hear a little crack. That's mine gone! Dad, too, shakes his head, but Mam pushes out her tongue and there, perched on the tip, is the Polo mint, still in one piece.

When he goes to buy the ice cream, Mam insists that we, too, deserve some for having to suffer her in silence. There's no longer any need for the indigestion tablets. The Mersey is between us and Mrs Pearson and we are free to begin our holiday.

*   *   *

I know now why Auntie Annie insisted on coming to the park with us. We are led to a bench, for it's here that her Benjy gives his daily performance and it has to be seen to be believed. Benjy is a corgi whose legs have shrunk due to carrying such a huge belly, the latest in a whole line of corgis all killed by kindness.

We are told to stand some distance away and to keep quiet so as not to disturb Benjy. She sits on the bench, lifts him beside her, and starts singing, out of tune and in a high-pitched voice. Benjy listens for a few moments, his head on one side, and then joins in, yelping and howling.

'That dog's in pain,' my mother says, in a loud voice.

Auntie Annie stops to give him a piece of chocolate and scowls at Mam saying that of course he isn't and hasn't she ever heard a dog singing before?

'Is that what you call it?' Mam mutters.

Dad gives her a warning glance, for Auntie Annie is very sensitive, especially where corgis are concerned. Many pieces of chocolate later, the howling comes to a stop. I pat Benjy and tell him what a clever boy he is and I'm given what's left of the chocolate bar. He's so exhausted that he has to be carried all the way home.

Back in our small stuffy room, with its dark, heavy furniture and its one window looking out on a narrow back alley and lavatories and dustbins, Mam says that Auntie Annie should be reported to the RSPCA, for dogs are meant to be able to move around on their own four legs and should not be forced to perform in public. When I say that Benjy reminds me of the Reverend, Dad starts laughing. For a moment, I'm afraid Mam is going to tell him off, for she believes that ministers of religion should be respected, but my father's laughter is as catching as flu and soon all three of us are at it. There's a knock at the door and we hear Mrs Pearson's voice. She's probably telling us to be quiet, for it says in the rules that there is to be no unnecessary noise after eight o'clock, but it doesn't matter any more. There are only two days left and we're going to make the most of them. Then it's good-bye Liverpool and miserable old Pearson; Auntie Annie, who believes that the way to a dog's heart is through its stomach, and poor Uncle Bob who will never be killed through kindness.

*   *   *

I never thought I'd miss Standard Four. At first, I couldn't understand why, for I should be counting my blessings. It took me days to realize that what I missed were the windows. Although there wasn't much to be seen through them except the yard and the high wall between us and the boys' school, it was comforting to know that the world outside was still there. The windows in Standard Five are so high up in the walls that you can only see the sky, which is always grey. The room is much smaller and the desks so close together that even Miss Jones, who has no bosom and no behind, has to walk sideways, which she does all day, every day.

Last night in bed, as I imagined her bumping into people on the street because of looking the other way, I made up a rhyme about her:

Said a teacher called Jones, 'Excuse me
for being where I shouldn't be,
    but I've lost the knack
    to go forward or back
without going sideways, you see'.

Eleanor, who is the same width all round, made a bee-line for the back row the moment we entered the classroom, but was stopped before she could do any damage and ordered to sit in the front. Everyone else was given a choice, but I was so busy trying to think why I missed Standard Four that I left it too late.

That's why I'm sitting in the front row, next to Eleanor. She thinks I stayed back deliberately to be near her, and so do all the others. I've been chosen monitor of the week. Miss Jones probably feels sorry for me, for being regarded as Eleanor's friend will ruin my chance of making something of myself, but I'd rather she didn't because the first thing I have to do is fetch the register from Standard Four.

I suppose what I see on Miss Hughes's face could be called a smile. Absence may make her heart grow fonder, but not mine. She keeps me waiting, checking to see if the register is correct. I stand facing the windows. Everything is as it should be, with different shades of grey and dark corners that the light can't reach, but it doesn't make me feel any better. Miss Hughes gives me the register and our hands touch. I remember these hands breaking the chalk in half and pushing me against the iron peg, and I can't wait to get back to Standard Five.

This room, where you can only see the sky, is probably the best place for the Scholarship year. We are given copy-books instead of slates, so that mistakes cannot be rubbed out and forgotten. There are spelling tests and dictation and comprehension, which means understanding, most of it in English, for everyone knows you can't get on in the world without it. If numbers didn't matter I'd be well on my way to wherever it is we are supposed to go, but they do. Who wants to spend ages working out how long a train journey takes when you can look it up in the time-table? Yesterday, I was left with the one sheep which didn't belong in any of the fields and today with a piece of cake which no one seemed to want. Maggie Pritchard would have no trouble finding room for the sheep with the other ninety-nine, and Porky Pugh would soon make the piece of cake disappear, but numbers can't be rescued or eaten.

Miss Jones tells us we have to keep our noses to the grindstone this year. I have no idea what a grindstone is but it sounds very painful. Eleanor puts up her hand. She wants to know if we have to bring one to school. Miss Jones explains it's just another way of saying we have to work hard. Why do teachers always have to do that? I suppose they must, for if we understood everything the first time they would all be on the dole. I'll look up the word in my dictionary tonight and write it down in the notebook with all the other sayings that mean something else like 'all hands to the deck', 'empty vessels make most noise' and 'a bad worker blames his tools'. And perhaps, if I'm not too tired from all the hard work, I'll write a verse about noses and grindstones, for I must not bury my talent although it's Scholarship year.

*　　*　　*

This morning, when I called to tell Ann I'd be working in Bethesda cemetery with my father today, I still hadn't finished the verse because I couldn't find the right word to rhyme with 'smell', although there must be at least ten to choose from.

'Wouldn't you rather go to the library and have ice and port in Taddies?' Ann asked.

That's what we do every Saturday afternoon. The library is at the far end of town, and because Ann can't pass any shop window it takes us an hour to get there. It's a waste of time, for what's the point of looking if you can't afford to buy? Then, when we at last reach the library, she complains if I spend more than ten minutes choosing a book.

Ice and port is my only treat and I try to make it last as long as possible, but Ann has got into the habit of gulping everything down before Porky Pugh can get at it. I pretend not to notice when she says, 'Excuse me' and burps behind her hand, for it isn't her fault. Every Saturday I tell her she can go if she wants to, but she never does for she wouldn't want to be seen all alone.

Today she'll have no choice, unless she finds

someone to tag on to, which is something I would be too proud to do. When I told her I'd rather work than walk the street, and that a picnic is as good as ice and port any day she said, in Miss Hughes's disgusted voice,

'You can't have a picnic in a graveyard.'

Mrs Pugh struggled in from the back-yard, carrying the washing, and there, on top, were the woollen combinations which cover Mr Pugh from his neck to his ankles. I remembered watching them slide between the rollers the day I was sent to apologize for saying that Ann and her mother could go to hell.

'I've got it!' I shouted.

As I rushed out of the house I could hear Mrs Pugh saying,

'You'd better stay away from that Helen. It could be catching.'

By the time I reached our front gate, the verse was finished:

> Hard work is all very well
> but it can be 'h' 'e' double 'l'
>   for a grindstone held close
>   can rub off your nose
> and leave you with no sense of smell.

Mam says, 'Have a good day and don't forget to wash the jam pot before putting the flowers in', and off we go to catch a bus. The flowers are Mam's idea, as they will give the finishing touch. At first, there was nothing in Dad's workshop but a large slab of stone delivered from the quarry, but then he drew leaves and flowers and measured out letters and brought them all to life with his hammer and chisel. I had to keep quiet so as not to disturb his concentration, for one slip could ruin everything. When he had finished the last letter he stepped back and I could tell he was proud of his work, although he doesn't like making his living out of the dead. When every speck of dust had been blown and wiped away, he told me to fetch the gold leaf. It comes in a small cardboard box and must not be touched by hand. I've never believed in fairies and wizards, but watching my father fill in the letters with a paintbrush dipped in gold was pure magic.

Dad had hired a lorry to take the gravestone to the cemetery and it's there waiting for us. The stone has to be washed and scrubbed, and it's my job to carry the water. I take a short cut to the tap, without realizing that there are graves underneath the grass until I trip over one of them. I say I'm sorry and go round the long way. These little mounds of grass belong to them, whoever they are, and I wouldn't like anyone to walk into my bedroom without permission.

I must have made at least eight journeys and I'm aching all over. I hold the bucket under the tap and hope that this is the last time. Back I go again, the bucket getting heavier with every step I take. Ann will be half-way to the library by now, trying to pretend that she doesn't mind being on her own.

'Let's have our picnic,' Dad says. 'I think we've earned it, don't you?'

'What's that verse in the Bible about having to work for your food?' I ask.

'In the sweat of your face you shall eat bread.'

Food tastes much better when you've earned it. I think of Ann, who hasn't done a day's work in her life and has no sense of taste because she has to swallow without chewing. When I tell my father what she said about eating a picnic in a graveyard he says,

'I don't suppose many people would fancy it.'

I was going to ask, 'Why not?' but I think I know what the answer would be. I feel a shiver inside, as if someone has switched off the sun.

We'll call at Auntie Lizzie's before we go home because the house is opposite the bus stop. Nain Manod will reach for Dad's photo and move it to the front row, rubbing the glass with her apron saying, 'If I'd known you were coming I'd have washed your face.' Auntie Lizzie will ask if we'd like a boiled egg with our tea as she does every time we call and Nain Manod will remind her, as she did the last time, that they haven't got any eggs, for Mrs Jones has stopped laying. Auntie Lizzie will smile and say, 'That's nice', for it's Sunday tomorrow and that means switching off to save the battery.

I wonder if Auntie Lizzie has ever felt a shiver inside. I shouldn't think so. Her heart is like a hot water bottle that is never allowed to get cold. Nain Manod was right when she said God broke the mould when He made Lizzie because everyone I know, even my father, can't seem to stop that happening and my heart needs refilling far too often.

The picnic is over and it's back to work. Dad sets the kerb-stones, two long ones at the sides and a shorter one at the foot, and fills in the space in between with chippings. The sun, which is still there, makes them glisten like frost. I wash the jam jar, even scraping the inside with my nails, before adding the finishing touch. We stand back to admire our work, pride in a job well done making us feel warm inside once again.

* * *

It's Friday evening and we're all sitting in the vestry. The Reverend's face is flushed and he finds it difficult to breathe because his dog collar is pressing against his treble chin. He's afraid we won't be able to answer any of the questions in the Scripture Examination and that he will be blamed for our lack of knowledge. My mother, as Sunday School supervisor, has handed out writing paper and pencils and rubbers, but David John has got his own fountain pen and a bottle of black ink in case it runs dry. He says Robert John let him borrow the pen for good luck.

Edwin keeps looking towards the door to make sure his mother is still standing in the porch. The Reverend has let Barbara and Betty sit together as he finds it easier to allow the rules to be broken than to separate them. Barbara, or Betty, asks Janet, 'What are you doing here?', and when she says 'Don't know' we all laugh except Llinos Wyn who's already started writing although we haven't yet seen the questions.

They are kept in a large envelope which is not to be opened until six o'clock, a rule the Reverend doesn't intend breaking. I peer over Llinos Wyn's shoulder. She's written her name and address and is now adding 'Wales, Great Britain, The World'.

When the clock strikes six, the Reverend is too nervous to open the envelope and he passes it to my mother saying,

'Keep your fingers crossed, Mrs Owen.'

He should have more faith in us, being a minister of religion.

Mam now shares out the slips of paper. She smiles, for she knows I am capable of answering the questions, whatever they are.

Edwin's mother knocks on the porch door. It's time for his medicine, which must be given on the hour. The Reverend lets her in. She takes a spoon from her pocket, wrapped in tissue paper, and tells Edwin to 'Open wide'. They both swallow together. She gives him a sweet to suck, glances at the question paper, and whispers, 'Locusts and wild honey', before returning to the porch. At least he'll get one answer right and so will Barbara and Betty, who have written 'bread of heaven' and have to rub the words out.

Llinos Wyn has stopped writing and is complaining

that her hand hurts. Janet has filled one page, but when my mother asks if she wants some more paper she says, 'Don't know'. She's given one and soon she has filled that as well. Betty and Barbara glare at her; for to say you don't know when you do is something they've never done, although they often say they do when they don't.

I can see Llinos Wyn has forgotten the names of Jesus's disciples. She's only gone as far as James and John and added 'etc'.

'No copying, Helen,' says the Reverend.

It's my mother's turn to glare. She assures him there's no need for me to copy anyone and that such an insinuation isn't worthy of a man of the cloth.

Edwin's mother has been called again, for he needs to go to the toilet. The Reverend insists on going with them, but when they return Edwin has secured himself another mark. What was it this time, loaves and fishes or water into wine? Although she looks as if butter wouldn't melt in her mouth, Edwin's mother can be very devious.

I've answered all the questions and I haven't used the rubber once. I sit up and look around. Barbara and Betty are playing oxo, Edwin is waving to his mother and Janet is still writing all she knows.

'Time's up,' shouts the Reverend.

As Llinos Wyn hands in her two pages, half of which is no good at all, she screams and points towards the back. All I see is a pair of black hands.

'What have you done, David John?' cries my mother.

111

'I'll kill that Robert John,' he mutters.

'Remember the Commandments,' booms the Reverend.

David John should have known better than to trust his brother. I suppose it was his idea of a joke to give him a pen that leaked. He's always playing tricks on people, and his grandmother – who lives with them – is too frightened to move if he's around. David John's face, when I see it, is also black, with little threads of white showing through. Barbara and Betty start giggling and one of them says,

'We've got two cry babies now.'

Edwin bursts into tears and his mother comes rushing in.

'What have you done to him?' she asks.

'I'll kill him,' David John shouts, jumping to his feet.

Edwin's mother grabs hold of Edwin, saying that she will be going straight to the police station to report David John for threatening her son's life. When my mother tries to calm her, the Reverend says,

'Leave everything to me, Mrs Owen.'

He ushers them out. I can hear him telling Edwin's mother that he will see them home and they can discuss this over a nice cup of tea.

'Will they put David John in prison?' Llinos Wyn asks.

'Don't know,' says Janet.

Barbara and Betty give her looks that could kill, and one of them says that David John would be doing everyone a favour by getting rid of his brother.

112

'I haven't done nothing,' he cries.

'You should say "I haven't done anything".'

Llinos Wyn, who didn't even know the names of Jesus's disciples, has the cheek to correct him.

My mother, who has been collecting the papers and putting them in the envelope, says,

'Of course he hasn't. David John would never harm anyone.'

'I could if I wanted to,' he mumbles.

I know how he feels. That Robert John has got a lot to answer for. If it wasn't for him we'd be on our way home by now and Mam would be bursting to tell my father how well I've done.

As they leave, Barbara and Betty shout,

'We'll bring you some nuts, David John, and feed you through the bars.'

'You won't be allowed to,' says Llinos Wyn. 'They're only given bread and water in prison.'

Mam tells them not to be silly. 'Stupid' is the word I'd have used, for boys can't be sent to prison, especially for something they haven't done. It's Edwin's mother who should be punished for encouraging her son to cheat in a Scripture Examination.

We meet the Reverend on the way home. He's carrying a biscuit tin and looking very pleased with himself.

'All sorted, Mrs Owen,' he says. 'And how did you manage without me?'

Mam decides that such a question isn't worth answering.

'Did you enjoy your tea?' she asks.

'It was just what I needed. It's been quite a night, hasn't it?'

'Never again,' mutters my mother, sounding exactly like Miss Evans Next Door.

'God will see us through. Have a biscuit, Helen.'

'No, thank you.'

Edwin's mother bakes her own biscuits because shop ones give Edwin indigestion, and I don't want any hand-outs from a woman who looks as if butter wouldn't melt in her mouth but is more than willing to cheat and report innocent boys to the police.

'I think I'll have one, to help me along.'

Off he goes, munching. He seems to have forgotten his fear that he would be blamed for our lack of knowledge. When the results arrive, and my high marks are read out, he will probably take all the credit and even God won't get a mention.

*   *   *

My father is feeling very sorry for himself. Mam has done all she can and her patience is running low. She tells him to go to bed and sweat it out. He refuses, saying it's a well-known fact that people die in their beds.

'It's only a cold, for goodness' sake,' Mam says.

'Colds can kill,' Dad mumbles, reaching for his second box of tissues.

When Mam says, 'I don't suppose you feel like eating', he reminds her of the old saying, 'Feed a cold and starve a fever'. Anyway, this cold hasn't yet reached his stomach and he'd better build up his strength before it does.

Although he says his throat feels like emery paper when he swallows, Dad manages to get it all down.

'Do you feel better now?' I ask.

'I wish I did,' he sighs.

Mam, whose patience has now run out, fetches his hat and coat and tells him he'll be in time for evening surgery if he hurries.

'I can't,' Dad cries. 'I've never been there, and I never will.'

She throws the coat and hat on a chair and says it's either Doctor Jones or bed. He sighs again and goes upstairs, dragging his feet and clutching a box of tissues and a packet of Polo mints. Mam settles herself by the fire, letting the warmth soothe her, and says,

'Peace and quiet, at last.'

I'm on my way to the surgery to fetch a bottle of the brown medicine which will cure Dad in no time at all, according to my mother.

Although it's only a quarter to, and surgery doesn't start until five, the place is already full of people who prefer to wait before rather than after. Many of them live alone and they make the most of their time here, discussing constipation and the runs, in-growing toe nails, piles and housemaids' knees.

I knock on the door in the wall. It slides to one side and Miss Edwards peers out. Before I can tell her why I'm here she says, 'Number 14', and the door is slid back.

You can almost hear the germs buzzing around like flies. Edwin's mother is here, huddled in a corner, a thick woollen scarf covering her mouth and nose. She shivers every time anyone sneezes or coughs. She'll be a nervous wreck by the time she gets to see the doctor. Annie Griffiths, who's a member of our chapel, asks me, 'And what's wrong with you, Helen?' and when I whisper, 'It's my father', she turns to the woman sitting next to her, who's here to have her corns treated and her ears syringed, and booms,

'Did you hear that, Madge? Richard Owen *cerrig beddi* is in a bad way.'

'Is it the dust?' Madge asks.

'No, it's only a cold,' I say, but my words fall on four deaf ears. They're off, discussing the dangers of spending hours in damp graveyards and breathing in dust that clogs the veins and settles around the heart.

When number 12 is called out, Annie shouts,

'It's you next, Madge. Remember to tell him about your ears,' and Madge says, as she waddles away,

'He'll have them off in no time.'

As I pass the little door in the wall on my way to what is called the consulting room, it slides open. Miss Edwards gives me a card with my name on and says with a sniff,

'You don't look ill to me.'

Doctor Jones tells me how nice it is to see a young face. He must be sick and tired of wrinkled old faces and creaking bones.

'How old are you now, Helen?' he asks.

'I was ten in August. I'll be going to the County School next year.'

'Good heavens. Children seem to grow up much quicker these days.'

I tell him I'd rather stay as I am and he says,

'That's exactly how I felt when they made me wear long trousers that covered my knees.'

'Knees are ugly things,' I say, pulling down my skirt to cover my own.

'I was very fond of mine.'

We talk about school. He, too, had a teacher who picked on him. She's now a patient of his and the boot is on the other foot, which means he could let her suffer, which he won't because his job is to heal. I tell him about the Christmas party and my Aunt Kate being sent home and how Miss Evans put up the rent because of the broken window. He agrees with me that blaming others makes people feel better and that revenge, as he well knows, is a terrible thing.

Miss Edwards knocks on the door and calls,

'Another five to go, Doctor.'

He reaches for his stethoscope and says,

'Let's have a listen to this chest of yours.'

I try to explain there's nothing wrong with me. It's very difficult to talk when you have to breathe in and out but I manage to get the words out at last.

'And what was it your mother wanted?' he asks.

'A bottle of the brown medicine.'

Doctor Jones smiles and says,

'That should do the trick.'

He writes out the prescription, tells me not to be in too much of a hurry to grow up, for knees are nothing to be ashamed of, and to warn my father that he must finish the whole bottle or face the consequences.

There's another long wait at the chemist's. Madge is here, leaning against the counter, telling everyone in a very loud voice that she hopes the new man from South Wales making up the prescriptions knows what he's doing, for they're not the same as us, down there. I ask her very politely if she's had them off. She tells me there's no need to shout and will I please get her a chair, for she's just had her bunions seen to and can't be expected to stand.

When I go through to the back, the new chemist is counting out some pills. He's startled when he hears my voice, swears, and says this is not a furniture shop and that he'll have to start all over again. At least, that's what I think he said. It's no wonder Madge is worried, for how can a man who is so easily frightened and can't speak proper Welsh be trusted? I return without a chair, but Madge is on her way out saying she'll wait until tomorrow morning when Boots will be open, for it's better to be safe than sorry.

As I leave, twenty minutes later, I meet my mother on her way to the chip-shop.

'How's Dad?' I ask.

'Just the same, but things will soon change.'

'Doctor Jones said he has to finish the whole bottle.'

'Make sure you tell him.'

And off she goes, looking very pleased with herself.

Dad is huddled under the bedclothes, pretending to be asleep. When I tell him I've got his medicine, and that Doctor Jones said he's to take it all or face the consequences, he opens one eye and peers at the bottle.

'I don't need it,' he says. 'It's only a cold, here today, gone tomorrow.'

'But colds can kill.'

I remove the cap and fill it to the brim with the brown liquid. It looks and smells horrible, and by the time he manages to sit up I feel quite sick.

'Open wide,' I say, pressing my lips together.

But he doesn't, and most of the medicine dribbles down his chin. He reaches for a Polo mint to take away the taste and asks where my mother is, for she hasn't been to see him for hours. When I tell him she's gone to the chip-shop, he pushes back the bedclothes and swings his legs over the side saying he won't be able to sleep tonight if he stays in bed any longer.

We've finished our supper and Dad said it was the best he had ever tasted. Mam tells me to fetch the bottle from upstairs, for the medicine is to be taken every three hours.

'There's no need,' Dad says. 'I'm feeling much

better now. It's true what they say about feeding a cold.'

*　　*　　*

Another Christmas is approaching and Miss Evans has informed my mother that she will sacrifice her piano playing in order to concentrate on the poor children who are in danger of being led astray by a shepherd who can't see his own feet, let alone the narrow path. Instead of having a party we are to perform a Christmas pageant, for Jesus's birth deserves better than jelly and sandwiches and pin-the-tail-on-the-donkey. For once, Mam agreed with her, seeing it as an opportunity for me to show what I'm capable of.

We are all made to stay behind after Sunday School, everyone except the Reverend who was very relieved to be told he wouldn't be needed. After the last Band of Hope, he was too exhausted to move and would have spent the night in the vestry if Mr Price hadn't heard him snoring just as he was about to switch off the lights. Miss Evans shares out the copies and warns us that we must treat them with care and respect. They have our names on them, and the parts we are to play. I'm to be the inn-keeper's wife. Mam won't be at all pleased, for the few words I have to say will hardly give me a chance to prove myself.

Barbara and Betty, as two of the wise men, will be wearing crowns instead of tea-towels, although they'll still have to bow their heads before Llinos Wyn, who is no longer an angel but Mary, the mother of Jesus. When he saw he was to play Joseph, David John threw his copy on the floor and said that no way was he going to be married to Llinos Wyn. A purple-faced Miss Evans called him an ungrateful boy, for it was a great privilege to be asked to play the part of Jesus's father.

Betty and Barbara started giggling, and one of them said everyone knew Joseph was not the father and that Jesus was born from an actual infection. Llinos Wyn gave a loud shriek and ran out, shouting that she didn't want to be infected. I told Miss Evans I wouldn't mind being Mary, for I'd already had the measles, but all she said was,

'You'll never make a Mary, Helen Owen.'

When I got home, I asked Mam what she meant and she said it was probably revenge because of the broken window. I didn't bother learning my part. It was back to jelly and musical chairs, Madame Rees on the piano, and no Eleanor this time to put me to shame.

The first thing I see when I arrive at chapel the following Sunday is Llinos Wyn standing outside the vestry holding a huge cardboard box. I can't stop myself from asking,

'What have you got there?'

She opens the lid carefully and says,

'It's Baby Jesus.'

We are told to stay behind once again. Mam offers

to help, so that she can make sure I'm given a fair deal, but Miss Evans tells her she'll be called upon if and when she's needed. Barbara and Betty say they thought Christmas had been cancelled because Jesus could not be born without a mother, but it seems that Llinos Wyn has decided it's worth taking the risk of being infected.

Miss Evans holds up a large, ugly doll, its mouth wide open like Billy Jones. It lets out a shriek, exactly like Llinos Wyn. The noise startles Miss Evans and she drops the doll, but David John rushes forward and catches it. He grins, saying he's saved Jesus's life and that there *will* be a Christmas after all. We all clap and cheer. Llinos Wyn grabs the doll off David John without even thanking him and pushes a plastic bottle into its open mouth. Miss Evans smiles and says,

'Isn't she the perfect little mother?'

Edwin is to be the father, who is not really the father but chosen by God and Miss Evans. David John is now the inn-keeper, and that's fine by him. Betty and Barbara refuse to have anything to do with little Janet-don't-know, who is supposed to be the third wise man. When they say she'd make a better sheep, Miss Evans pretends she hasn't heard. I think she's afraid of them for they are both double her size, which means four against one.

When I read my part I put on a posh voice like Mrs Bevan, who owns the Royal Hotel, but Miss Evans tells me not to be a silly girl and to remember I'm only a poor inn-keeper's wife. It's a horrible feeling being called silly in front of everyone. I can hear Barbara and Betty giggling but when I look up, struggling to keep back the tears, I can see them pointing towards Llinos Wyn who has just arrived at the inn, the doll in her arms. Miss Evans tries to take it off her, saying that baby Jesus isn't born yet, but she won't let go. She squeezes the doll, and it pees all over her.

Mary has gone home with Baby Jesus in disgrace, having been called a naughty boy and given a smack, and Janet has taken her place. Edwin, who wanted to go to the toilet and can't, without his mother, has also left. When Betty or Barbara asks Janet if this is where the new king has been born she says, 'Don't know' and they both shout back, 'Of course it is, stupid!' Miss Evans now decides that Janet can be the inn-keeper's wife, as long as she lets him do the talking. I'm to be the third wise man with only three words to say and all because of a broken window. Revenge is a terrible thing.

Just as we are leaving, David John tells Miss Evans that his brother Robert John, who was absent today, is not allowed to take part in the pageant because of what he's done. We all wait for Miss Evans to ask what exactly he has done so that we'll know, but all she says is, 'What am I going to do now?' David John winks at me and asks if I'm ready to help poor Miss Evans out by being Herod. Barbara and Betty shout, 'Of course she is' and all the others agree, for it's past tea time and their stomachs are rumbling. Miss Evans sighs and hands me a new copy with 'King Herod – Helen Owen' written on it. I suppose I'll have to suffer for this, but just now I don't care.

When I ask David John as we walk home what it is that Robert John has done he grins and says,

'Nothing. It's his fault for skiving. You'll look great in a crown and a beard, Helen.'

I'm not so sure about the beard, but I've got the best part and a chance to prove myself. If it wasn't Sunday, I'd give David John a kiss on the cheek to say 'thank you'. Perhaps I'd better not tell Mam how I got the part. I'll just say Miss Evans realized I deserved better, which isn't true, but should be.

*   *   *

It will probably be jelly and sandwiches and pin-the-tail-on-the-donkey again next Christmas, for Miss Evans has decided that the damage cannot be undone. We are already on our way to destruction, and we all know whose fault that is.

The pageant was a disaster from beginning to end. There were two Josephs, one big and one small, because Edwin refused to take part unless his mother came too. When the big one asked if there was room at the inn, Janet said 'Don't know' and David John told her to go back inside and leave it to him. Llinos Wyn had hidden Baby Jesus under her cloak, ready to be born, and once they were in the stable she took him out and gave him a cuddle. He squealed, frightening little Joseph. Big Joseph took his hand and said, 'Say hello to your little brother'. Glenys Lloyd, the angel of the Lord, who was wearing her mother's wedding dress, tripped and fell and couldn't get up because her foot was caught in the hem. 'Don't be afraid,' she said, struggling to get free. 'I am the bringer of great joy', and down she went again. Miss Evans had to finish the message and the shepherds went off, leaving her lying there. 'That's what they call a fallen angel,' David John whispered. As I was strutting across the stage, the spitting image of King Herod, my beard slipped and I had to finish my speech with my mouth full of hairs. Mam said afterwards that to have carried on under such circumstances showed what I'm capable of.

We had to sing 'Away in a manger' without the piano, for Miss Evans had gone, muttering 'never again' as she went. If looks could kill, not one of us would have seen Christmas. The Reverend was so upset that he only managed to say, 'May the Lord be with you all, Amen'. I'm sure he needed Him more than we did. Mr Price said it wasn't his job to clear up the mess and disappeared through the door that leads to the chapel house. Edwin was crying because he didn't want a little brother, and the two wise men wanted their presents back, but Llinos Wyn refused, saying they belonged to Baby Jesus.

Five minutes later, they had all left, sniffling and shouting.

'Are you going to clear up, Mam?' I asked.

'No, I'm not,' she said. 'They can all go to . . .'

I finished the sentence for her. She clicked her tongue, and then smiled. As we were putting our coats on in the lobby she turned to me and said,

'Happy Christmas, Helen.'

'And a happy Christmas to you too, Mam,' I said, and off we went to celebrate our own Christmas.

*   *   *

Mam told me this morning to be extra careful not to annoy Miss Evans. When I asked, 'Has that Edgar James dumped her?' for there's been no sight or sound of him for weeks, Mam glared at me and said,

' "Dumped" is a word nice girls should never use.'

'Eleanor uses it all the time.'

'Which proves my point. And how did you know his name?'

'Mrs Morris number one told me. She said he'll have no choice but to marry Miss Evans.'

'Gossiping is another thing nice girls shouldn't do.'

I've known for a long time that I'm not one of the nice girls, for they don't hide bottles under their skirts and pour milk down the pan, or write naughty rhymes about teachers and ministers of religion, or hold hands with boys on Sunday School trips. It must be very boring to be one of them and having to remain in ignorance because finding things out for yourself is not allowed.

'Has he?' I asked again.

'That is none of our concern. Just mind your

manners and don't ask her how she is, whatever you do.'

'What am I supposed to say to her then?'

'Let her do the talking and agree with everything she says.'

'Even if I don't?'

'Especially if you don't. It would be better if you could keep out of her way for a few days.'

That meant going out the back way and keeping my head down as I passed the wall between us and next door. But this morning I was in such a hurry to get to the lavatory that I forgot, and there she was, hanging her washing on the line. Pink flannelette bloomers, reaching down to the knees, and thick lisle stockings had taken the place of the silk knickers and the see-through nylons. She must have seen me, but pretended not to and scuttled indoors as if I'd caught her doing something she shouldn't.

There was one way of finding out what had happened. Mrs Morris would tell me all I wanted to know and as I'm not one of the nice girls there was nothing to stop me. But I couldn't. I sat there for ages trying to think why. Mam knocked on the door and said that an outside lavatory wasn't made for reading in.

'I wasn't reading,' I said, as I followed her into the house. 'I was thinking about Miss Evans. Do you think we should ask her to tea?'

Mam looked at me as if I had more than one screw missing and said that would only make things worse.

'Why?' I asked. 'She must be feeling very lonely.'

'And whose fault is that?'

'Hers, I suppose.'

'Exactly. She could have destroyed that poor man's life, chasing after him and making a nuisance of herself.'

'But he saw the light, as Dad did with Miss Hughes.'

'That's enough!' Mam said in a tone of voice that would put the fear of God into anyone. She stormed off to the kitchen saying she had better things to do, and closed the door behind her.

I'm walking down our road with only my shadow for company. I left by the front door for I didn't want Miss Evans to think we'd turned our backs on her. I remember how she has made me suffer because of the broken window and I can't understand why I should feel sorry for her when she has no one to blame but herself.

I decide to call on Ann, although I'm not supposed to be there until this afternoon. Mrs Pugh opens the door, wearing her wrap-over apron and smelling of carbolic soap.

'Ann's very busy just now,' she says.

Another door is closed and I'm left with nowhere to go and no one to talk to. Mr Pritchard, Next Door, leaning on the front gate and puffing away at his pipe, which he's not allowed to smoke in the house, smiles at me and says,

'Isn't it a fine day?'

I remember the morning Miss Evans ran to catch up with me, with her hair hanging loose and wearing her Sunday coat; a miserable, ugly morning when she could smell and feel Spring in the air and believe all was well with the world. She won't be able to do that, ever again. She'll be all alone in the house her great-grandfather built all those years ago, with only her father's walking stick hanging on the hall-stand as a warning to strangers. I walk on because I have nothing better to do. A cloud has passed over the sun and even my shadow is no longer there.

*   *   *

I've added Uncle Jack's and Aunt Kate's names to my prayer because no one else will remember them. I suppose I should include my grandmother, but it's probably too much to expect of God, who has already spent over eighty years looking after her.

Tonight, I left out the 'me' and added another name. I wouldn't want God to think I can do without him, but I'm not sure if I have the right to ask him to take care of six of us. What if everyone else did the same? But it will only be for a few nights, and Margaret needs him even more than I do just now.

I will never forgive them for ruining what should be one of the happiest days of my life. The results of the Scholarship had arrived and Miss Hughes and Miss Lloyd read out the names of those who had passed and made us line up in order. There would be no prize for guessing who came first. Megan-Williams-who-can-do-no-wrong had done it again. We were kept waiting in suspense while they, smiling all over their faces like a pair of Cheshire cats, their bosoms swelling with pride, told her what a clever girl she was, which she already knew.

'How do we feel, girls?'

'Proud, Miss Lloyd.'

Next in line came Elsie, second-in-all-subjects-that-count. I wasn't far behind, but the smiles were starting to fade a bit by then. When Ann and Eleanor's names were called there were only a few left. Then, suddenly, the smiles disappeared. Margaret, the only one who had failed, was made to stand at the end of the line, with a gap between her and the rest. I could feel my stomach churning, the bile rising to my throat. She looked so lonely standing there. I should have gone to her, told her that it didn't matter. But it did matter to them. She had let the school down and was a great disappointment to those who had dedicated their lives to giving us girls the best education possible. And they had punished her by setting her apart as if she had committed some crime.

I was sick in the gutter on the way home. Ann, who was crying for herself, said it was a disgusting thing to do. I told her that what had happened in school was far more disgusting than puking into the gutter. She accused me of being big-headed and blaming Margaret for failing when she couldn't help being a bit slow.

'It's what they did to her,' I cried. 'How could they be so cruel?'

She just stared at me and asked,

'Was it Megan and the others? I didn't see them doing anything.'

She is really the most stupid person I know. Margaret has more brains in her little finger than Ann has in the whole of her body.

I was as white as a sheet and smelt of sick when I arrived home and Mam had to catch hold of a chair to steady herself before saying,

'Never mind, you tried your best.'

When I told her that I had passed, she went straight into the kitchen to fetch the cake she had baked and asked would I prefer white or pink icing.

Perhaps Margaret's mother had baked a cake. What would she do now? She couldn't afford to throw the cake into the dustbin. If it was Ann, Porky Pugh could have scoffed the lot and there would be no tell-tale crumbs left, but Margaret has no brother or sister and the cake, if there was one, would have to be eaten.

When Dad came home, he took one look at the cake, decorated with little pink blobs which were meant to be flowers, and said,

'So we're celebrating, are we?'

'I'm not,' I mumbled, fighting to keep the tears back.

Margaret didn't cry. She just stood there, staring at the floor, as if she didn't know what was happening. My father didn't know, either. He whispered something to my mother and she smiled proudly and said,

'Of course she did. She isn't feeling too well, that's all, with all the worrying and the excitement.'

'Would you have baked a cake if I'd failed?' I asked.

'What a silly question.'

'Would you?'

'It was ready when you came home, wasn't it?'

Had Margaret's mother been waiting, as she had, before putting the icing on? Would my mother have thrown it away, not caring what it had cost? I would never know, because I had passed.

'How did the others do?' my father asked, drowning his tinned peaches with evaporated milk.

'We all passed except Margaret.'

'Poor girl. Isn't she the one who's good at drawing?'

'That doesn't count.'

I took a piece of cake to please my mother and wrapped it in my handkerchief when she wasn't looking. When I came up to bed, I broke it into little pieces and threw them out of the window. There won't be a crumb left by morning. It should have been a special tea, and it was for my Mam and Dad. I couldn't tell them what had happened.

There's nothing I can do but ask God to remember Margaret. I did think of asking Him to assure her it doesn't matter and that she has her own special talent, but He'll probably put it better than I can. Perhaps Margaret will become a famous artist one day and Miss Lloyd will boast how she and the others had believed in giving their girls the best education in all subjects. The sick smell has disappeared after a good wash but the disappointment and anger will stay with me for a long time, perhaps for ever.

* * *

I've been summoned next door, for Miss Evans is indisposed with what she calls summer flu. She's not a pretty sight at the best of times but if he-who-had-done-it could see her now he'd be so relieved that he saw the light.

She shuffles around the room, wheezing and snuffling as she goes, and not even bothering to use a handkerchief.

'It's terrible to be all alone in the world, Helen,' she complains between a sneeze and a cough, which is a very ungrateful thing to say considering that I'm standing here, waiting for my orders. Not only that, but putting myself in danger, for coughs and sneezes spread diseases.

Wanting to make my escape, I ask what she wants me to do. She clucks her tongue at my impatience and points to the shopping list on the table. It's lying on an open newspaper and the first thing I see is Megan Williams beaming up at me, looking very pleased with herself. I decide to ignore it, but Miss Evans is at my elbow, breathing her germs all over me.

'Isn't she a clever girl?' she says, smiling for the first time today.

There's only one answer to that and I'm not going to give it. I don't want to be reminded of that afternoon when Margaret was made to suffer and Megan Williams was clapped and cheered and paraded from classroom to classroom for having the highest marks in the County.

Miss Evans showers me with some more germs as she says,

'Her parents and the school must be so proud of her.'

'How do we feel, girls?'

'Proud, Miss Lloyd.'

She's now saying what a delight it will be to teach her. No matter how hard I try, I'll never be the cause of pride or pleasure.

I pick up the shopping list. Miss Evans has printed the prices opposite every item. She now adds it all up and gives me the exact money. Why doesn't she get the star pupil to run errands for her? There would be no need to draw a list or note the prices, for She-who-can-do-no-wrong remembers and knows it all.

It seems that I am not going to be allowed to forget Megan Williams, for as I wait my turn in the Co-op she walks past, looking straight ahead as if expecting someone to hold the door for her. She's had a perm and is wearing a new summer dress and shoes to match. The woman next to me nudges her friend and says,

'Look at her. Isn't she a proper little madam?'

'Too much attention if you ask me.'

'Brains aren't everything.'

When I get to the counter I tell the women that they can have my turn. I'm thanked and complimented on my nice manners, so different from some they could mention. I have a long wait while they argue about the 'divi', but it's been worth it for when I get there what's left of the bread is being sold at half price. Brains may get you your picture in the paper, but just now I'd rather have money in my pocket.

* * *

Dad had been looking forward to spending a week in Liverpool but my mother said that her idea of a holiday did not include a sour-faced landlady and a singing corgi, so he went out and bought three train tickets. They were called 'runabout tickets'. The train did the running about. We just sat there, staring through dirty windows and hoping we would be on time to catch the connections from Llandudno Junction.

The first day was a disaster. We had to wear our plastic macks, buttoned up to our chins, and the three of us were wet, cold and miserable even before we reached the station. Mam had insisted on wearing her best shoes and had to take them off on the train because her feet were already killing her. Dad teased her, holding his nose between finger and thumb, and asking, 'What's that bad smell?' She glared at him and said that she would rather have stayed at home, and whose stupid idea was this, anyway. It was agony putting the shoes on again, for her and for us. She refused to take my father's arm when we left the train, hobbled across the platform, and into the Ladies. My father and I stood there, waiting, as the train for Llandudno pulled out of the station.

'Shall we go back on the next train?' my father asked when she emerged at last, with red eyes and a powdered nose.

'And since when have we been able to afford throwing money away?' she said. 'I could do with a cup of tea, if that's all right with you.'

The tea, when it came, didn't please her. It was too strong and left a bad taste in the mouth, but she supposed it was better than nothing. As soon as she had finished, she got up and said,

'Well, what are we waiting for? We're here now, so let's make the best of it.'

By then, it was impossible to make the best of anything. We spent the afternoon in Llandudno, where there was no need to wear plastic macks. Dad and I went to the amusements on the pier but we felt too guilty to enjoy ourselves, thinking of Mam sitting all alone on a bench, nursing her aching feet. When we returned to her, she had her shoes off and was holding her face up to the sun. She smiled at us and said,

'Aren't you glad you came?'

To say we were would have been a lie, so we held

our tongues. The chips we had on the way back to the station were thick and greasy but Mam ate them all and told me off for wasting good food.

I went to bed that night thinking that I never wanted to see the inside of a train again. But we were off again the next morning, Mam wearing her old shoes and Dad carrying a bag holding a flask of tea, sandwiches, and three plastic macks, just in case.

For the rest of the week, we spent hours on the train, being carried from one place to another. The macks stayed where they were and the sun followed us wherever we went. There were castles to be seen and admired, the marble church at Bodelwyddan, the smallest house in the world on Conwy quay, the monument to Daniel Owen, the novelist, in Mold, and all taken back with us safe inside my little Brownie camera. We sat in the long grass, on stone walls and warm benches, and forgot that first day as we ate our sandwiches and drank tea that was exactly as tea should be. And on the Saturday, although worn out with all that running around, we all agreed that it had been a great idea.

*　　*　　*

I'm standing at the gate, waiting for my mother, when Miss Evans returns from doing her shopping. She must have recovered from her summer flu although her nose is still red from so much blowing and rubbing. Staring at the little brown case at my feet she says,

137

'Another holiday, Helen? Aren't you a lucky girl.'

For once I agree with her and I tell her, proudly, that I've been invited to stay at my uncle's farm for a whole week.

When she read the letter, Mam said it was good of Aunt Agnes to think of me, but that she couldn't even consider accepting the invitation for I was far too young to be sent away on my own. Seeing how upset I was, Dad tried to persuade her to reconsider, saying there's a first time for everything and that it would be ungrateful to refuse, but his words fell on stony ground. As he left for work he whispered, 'Leave it with me' and that's what I did for a long, sad day. When we were having supper Mam said in a tight little voice that as my father, being head of the household, obviously thought it was right and proper to send an eleven year-old girl miles away from home on her own she had no choice but to accept Aunt Agnes's invitation, but against her better judgment.

So it's thanks to Dad that I'm standing here now. Miss Evans is saying she's surprised my mother has agreed to this and that she hopes I will reward her trust in me. After warning me to respect the country code (whatever that is) and to remember at all times that I'm only a guest in my uncle and aunt's house, she disappears indoors.

My mother is very quiet as we walk towards the bus stop. I suppose I should tell her I'm sorry she isn't coming with me, but I'm not. There's already a long queue at the bus stop. Most of them will only

138

be going a few miles, but my journey is going to take two whole hours. I'm hoping someone will notice my case, but they are all too busy talking about the weather and the price of eggs.

Then Eleanor and her Nan join us. Eleanor is dragging a large case behind her and her Nan is carrying a bundle wrapped in brown paper. Eleanor's face is swollen as if she's got toothache. She's probably been caught doing something she shouldn't. There's nothing to stop her now; she's got all day to do it in. I certainly don't want to know what it is, so I tell her I'm away on holiday.

Her Nan gives me a look to kill and says,

'Eleanor is going to live with her Mam from now on.'

Eleanor starts shouting and screaming, 'No, I'm not' and 'Don't want to' over and over.

I hear a woman muttering, 'That girl needs a good spanking', but instead of telling her to shut up Eleanor's Nan puts her arms around her and they stand huddled together, as if they were the only two people left in the world. The woman now turns to me and asks,

'And where are you going to then?'

It's my mother who tells her and who answers her 'You're going to miss her, Mrs Owen' with 'A week will soon pass'. This sets Eleanor off again. I'm surprised at my mother. It was a cruel thing to say, for there will be no coming back for Eleanor.

As the bus arrives, I pat Eleanor on the arm and ask her if she'd like to sit with me.

'We'll wait for the next bus,' says her Nan. 'It'll give us a little more time together.'

I can't wait to get on the bus, away from Eleanor and her Nan's pain, for this should have been the most special day of my life. Mam hands me my case and tells me to avoid sitting on the wheel, not to read on the bus, and to open the window if it gets too stuffy. She seems to have realized what she said about a week soon passing, for she looks as if she's about to cry. I can't stand any more tears, so I give her a little wave before reaching into the case for my *School Friend*. By the time I lift my head we're half way down the main street and the woman who asked where I was going is saying,

'Your Mam will be counting the hours. A week can be a long time when you're missing someone.'

* * *

I have to go home this afternoon, for my new school tunic, ordered from the Co-op, has arrived. A letter came from Mam yesterday saying how much she and Dad have missed me. Auntie Agnes is in the dairy, churning as if her life depends on it. Perhaps it does. If you need to talk to Auntie Agnes you have to follow her around, in and out, up and down, but she's always switched on. I've never known anyone who can do so many things at the same time.

It's always cold in the dairy, but she doesn't seem to notice. Did my mother feel the cold when she stood here doing what Aunt Agnes is doing now?

I've tried to imagine her crossing the yard, her long skirt sweeping the cobbles, or sitting on a stool in the cowshed, her cheek pressed against the cow's flank, but it's no good. She doesn't belong here.

'And what are you going to do today?' asks Aunt Agnes, churning away.

'Say good-bye to everyone.'

I will probably go as far as the shop and the field behind the chapel where my friends from the village have their den, but the only one I want to say good-bye to is Aunt Dora, my mother's sister.

'You'll be back for your tea?'

'Yes, and thank you for having me.'

'You're always welcome here.'

Walking to the village leaves a lot of time for thinking, because there's nothing to see except fields and trees and they all look the same to me. All this green is making my eyes hurt and I can't wait to be back with my Mam and Dad, for when you miss someone a week is indeed a very long time.

When I come to my aunt's house and knock on the door, I'm told to come in, whoever I am. The room, with its one small window, is full of shadows. I walk through them to where my Aunt Dora is sitting, and they brush against my skin, soft and warm like Nick's feathers. In my grandmother's room, the shadows are as cold and sharp as slates.

We sit together on the settee in front of the fire. Aunt Dora is the only woman I know who smokes cigarettes. As we talk and laugh, I watch the wisps of smoke melting into the shadows. She has to stop talking every now and again to catch her breath and I pat her on the back when she starts coughing. This is the first time I've touched her and she, too, is soft and warm. My father would feel at home here. He'd puff at his pipe and the clouds of smoke would remain long after the wisps had melted. He'd tell some jokes which my mother thinks are unsuitable and Aunt Dora wouldn't click her tongue and say, 'That's enough now, Richard'.

I stay for as long as I can.

'I'm so glad you called,' Aunt Dora says.

And so am I.

My friends, too busy to leave whatever they're doing, call from their den,

'See you next summer.'

I don't suppose they'd care if I'd left without saying good-bye, but it doesn't matter, for Aunt Dora cared.

I buy some sweets to eat on the way back and keep some to give to Spot. He's waiting for me by the gate. He reminds me of Ann as he swallows the sweets without chewing. That's because he has no teeth left from chasing stones thrown by children who should know better. When I tell him I'm going home today he licks my hand. That's his way of showing he cares.

I wrap my arms around him and whisper in his ear,

'I'd take you with me if I could.'

But I wouldn't, for he belongs here.

*   *   *

The new tunic is too loose and too long for me but Mam says she won't bother with tucks and hems as I'll grow into it. This one would have enough room for Eleanor's bosom. She won't be coming to the County School although she passed the Scholarship. I saw her Nan on the street this morning. She scowled at me and said,

'Aren't you going to ask how Eleanor is?'

I was, but I didn't want to upset her.

'You've probably forgotten all about her.'

'No I haven't. Is she all right?'

'How can she be?'

She walked away, still scowling. There was nothing more to say. Eleanor has gone for good, back to a mother who left her with her Nan when she was a baby. Billy Jones will have to find someone else to snog and I will never know what they did behind Dwyryd Terrace.

The first thing I saw when I got home was the tunic, draped over the table. Mam was wringing out Dad's handkerchief ready to press the pleats. I told her she was wasting her time, for I had no intention of wearing it.

'You'll have to,' she said. 'It's too late to order another one now.'

I grabbed the tunic and threw it on the floor.

'Pick it up, Helen,' Mam said in a cold voice.

It was still lying there when my father came home from work. When Mam told him how stubborn I'd been, and that I was old enough to realize that clothes don't grow on trees, he picked it up and said,

'It would take a long time for her to grow into this.'

Mam stormed off to the Co-op to see if they had any more tunics in stock. Although it was my father who persuaded her to go, I knew he was annoyed with me for he doesn't like to see my mother upset. He waited in silence for her to return, was all smiles when she said she managed to get a smaller size, and left for a deacons' meeting without even saying good-bye to me.

I try the tunic on and Mam asks,

'Well, is that better?'

'It's perfect.'

'I suppose I could have altered the other one, but I'm no Dorcas.'

'Eleanor would never fit into this, Mam.'

'Poor Eleanor will never fit anywhere.'

'Miss Hughes said she was disgusted with her and she was sent to Coventry.'

'Why?'

'I don't know. She'd probably done something she shouldn't.'

I should say I'm sorry, but I'm not, for the first day in the County School will be bad enough without being made fun of and branded for ever as the one who was all tunic and no legs. It's so easy to hurt people and so hard to make them understand because they always think they know better and never feel the need to say sorry.

*   *   *

144

Ann is waiting for me by the gate. She's wearing a new blazer with the school badge sewn on the pocket.

'Why haven't you got your blazer on?' she asks.

I tell her it's far too warm to wear one and show her my leather satchel, which was a present from my father and has the letters H.O. stamped on, in gold. She'll probably have one just like it by the end of the week, but I'll have to do without a blazer. The money saved in the Co-op will be needed to buy a gabardine for winter.

We walk past our old school. Ann starts sniffing and says she wishes we were going back there. She stares at me with wide pink eyes when I say, 'I don't'. On the last day, I went to say good-bye to Mrs Edwards. The room looked exactly the same as it did when I couldn't wait to get there every morning. Mrs Edwards took a piece of paper from her desk. It was the poem I'd written about the fair. When I asked her if she'd like to keep it to remember me by, she smiled and said,

'I won't forget you, Helen.'

I don't suppose Miss Hughes will forget me either, but I'd give anything to be able to forget her.

I can hear voices coming from Dwyryd Terrace. Barbara and Betty are on their way.

'What's the matter with her?' one of them asks, noticing Ann's pink eyes and nose.

To save her from being labelled another *babi Mam*, I tell them she's got a cold. We walk on, Barbara and Betty on either side, telling us about the teachers who hate children and are only there for the money, about punishments and detentions, and school dinners that make you want to throw up. Ann, who believes every word, looks as if she's going to be sick any minute.

Before we reach the school gate, they say we'll have to find our own way from now on for they, as Third Formers, must not be seen in our company.

'I can't go in there,' Ann says, and off she goes the way we came.

I'm tempted to let her go but Mrs Pugh would probably blame me, as she usually does. I go after her and explain that Barbara and Betty are the biggest liars in town and make a habit of frightening people.

'I'm not frightened,' she says. 'I don't feel well. It must be the cold.'

It takes a lot of persuading but I manage to get her through the gate and up the drive. Megan and Elsie are standing outside the main door. They've both got blazers with badges on, and school ties. Megan informs us that we're to stay here until assembly, when we'll be told what form we're in.

'I know what to do,' I say, although I have no idea what assembly is or how to find it.

Ann, who's so stupid that she can't even pretend, says,

'I don't.'

And so we're stuck with them, listening to Megan saying how exciting this is.

146

When Ann tells them what Barbara and Betty said about the teachers, Megan says,

'I don't know how those two ever got into the County.'

I was just going to say that two heads are better than one when the bell rings and one of the teachers comes out and shouts,

'First Formers follow me.'

She leads the way along a corridor, her cloak flapping like wings, reminding me of a picture I saw in *The Children's Guide to Knowledge* of nasty little creatures called bats that hide in attics and church towers, called belfries, and eat spiders and mice.

Assembly is a huge room with a stage at one end. There are a lot more bats sitting there and one larger one standing and glaring down at us under thick, bushy eyebrows. He welcomes us but he doesn't look very friendly and I think perhaps Barbara and Betty could be right, after all. Our names are called out in alphabetical order and we have to stand in a line behind Mr Mathews, who's Form 1A, or Miss Evans, who's 1B. I cross my fingers and pray it's A.

God has looked after me for once. It's 1A and Mr Mathews, who's thin and droops as if he needs feeding and watering, like my Uncle Bob. I'm so relieved I've been spared that I missed hearing Ann's name being called. She's joining the other line. I hope she's not going to cry, for her own sake, although she didn't even thank me for saving her from Barbara and Betty.

We follow the two flapping figures, one to the right and one to the left. Megan, being Williams, is at the back, but she'll soon be in front.

Mr Mathews sighs as he tells us to copy down the time-table on the papers we've been given, divided up into squares. What we called sums is now called Maths, short for Mathematics, starting with a double lesson on Monday mornings, which is not the best way to start the week. There's Cookery for the girls and Woodwork for the boys and P.E., whatever that is, for everyone.

Megan and Elsie have desks in the front row, which no one else wanted. They whisper to one another. Mr Mathews, who's perched on a high chair behind his desk, bangs down the lid and says there is to be no talking in class. What would Miss Hughes and Miss Lloyd say if they knew their star pupils who-can-do-no-wrong had been told off on their very first day?

I wonder how Ann is getting on. She can be very tiresome at times, but I could do with her company now. Here, as in Standard Five, the windows are set high up in the walls but there's a tiny bit of blue showing through the bottom panes. The walls are bare and painted cream and the desks feel cold and damp. I suppose I'll get used to it, for this is where I'll have to spend the next eleven months – at least forty weeks, minus the holidays. That makes two hundred days. Mr Mathews sighs again. It's going to be a much longer wait for him, as he will probably be here until he retires. Realizing that someone else

148

is worse off should make me feel better, but it doesn't.

It's been a very long morning indeed, but at least it brings the total of days down to one hundred and ninety-nine and a half. As I wait for Ann, I watch the teachers heading for the canteen, flapping their wings and licking their lips:

> It's dinner time at the County,
> all the bats have flown from the belfry,
>   for they think that mice . . .

Before I get to the last two lines, Ann arrives, looking very miserable and no wonder, for the bad news she has to tell her mother will upset Mrs Pugh's routine for days.

'You were talking to yourself,' she says.

'No, I wasn't.'

'I saw your lips move. Mam says that's always a bad sign.'

'A sign of what?'

'You know.' And she touches her forehead.

I was going to tell her that it's better to be mad and in the A rather than sane and in B, but as we pass the canteen I can see Mr Morris hunched over a plateful of mashed potatoes with little pieces which could very well be mice-meat floating in the gravy. I close my lips tightly as I finish the rest of the verse in my head:

for they think that mice
taste ever so nice
with mashed potatoes and gravy.

*　　*　　*

As I was passing Eleanor's Nan's house this
afternoon on my way from school, I heard a strange
hissing sound. I stopped and peered over the gate,
and there was Eleanor, crouching behind the wall.

'What are you doing here, Eleanor?' I asked.

Instead of answering me, she asked if I knew
where her Nan was. I said she was probably at the
Institute, for it's jam and Jerusalem every Tuesday.

Eleanor scowled at me as if it was my fault her
Nan wasn't there.

'Get in here,' she hissed.

I was told to keep my head and my voice down
and we crouched there together.

'Don't you dare tell anyone you've seen me,' she
whispered.

'Why not?'

'Don't ask stupid questions.'

I wasn't going to stay there to listen to all these
don'ts and be called stupid, so I stood up and said I
had to go home, but Eleanor grabbed my arm and
promised to tell me everything if I'd keep her
company until her Nan returned.

She went on and on about her mother, who got up
to all sorts of things with one boyfriend after
another, but when I asked, 'What things?' she said I

wouldn't understand. She wasn't allowed in the house most evenings because her mother said she was cramping her style, whatever that means. The latest boyfriend had moved in as a lodger. Her mother made him a cooked breakfast every morning, but Eleanor only had a piece of toast, and she couldn't even swallow that because of having to look at his ugly mug across the table. Eleanor had refused to call him uncle, saying she was sick and tired of all these uncles and wanted her father. There was a terrible row and her mother had shouted,

'He never wanted you. I'd have got rid of you if it wasn't for your Nan, the interfering old witch!'

'Why did she want you back then?' I asked as soon as I could get a word in.

'She's a jealous cow, that's why.'

'You shouldn't say that about your mother.'

'I hate her. She only wanted to hurt my Nan by taking me away from her. I'll never go back there, ever, ever.'

I knew then that Eleanor had run away and wasn't supposed to be there at all. What if the police came looking for her? They could appear at any moment and they'd probably think I'd helped her to escape and take me to the police station for questioning.

'I can't stay any longer,' I said.

'But you promised. If you go now I'll never speak to you again.'

'I don't care. You shouldn't have run away, Eleanor.'

'And what do you know about it?' she shouted, forgetting that she wasn't supposed to be heard.

'You're just a spoilt little girl with a Mam and Dad who think the sun shines out of her ass.'

She gave me a push. I lost my balance and fell into the garden, which is all mud and no grass. As I lay there, I heard footsteps and the gate opening and thought how upset my parents would be when they had to fetch me from the police station, and the disgrace of everyone knowing. But it wasn't Sergeant Parry, forced to take his feet off the desk and do his duty, but Eleanor's Nan. She dropped her basket and rushed past me.

'What has she done to you, love?' she cried.

She knelt by Eleanor and wrapped her arms around her. I heard Eleanor saying,

'I've come home, Nan.'

'That's my girl,' her Nan said, holding her tightly.

'They won't take me away again, will they?'

'Over my dead body!'

They didn't notice me leaving. On the way home, I tried to think how to explain the mud on my tunic and decided to say that I'd tripped and fallen when playing hockey. Mam wouldn't be too pleased, because clothes cost money, but she'd probably say, 'Never mind. As long as you didn't hurt yourself', for she and Dad think the sun shines out of my bottom, which is a much nicer word than 'ass'.

*   *   *

We have two cinemas, which we call The Pictures, in our town. The Park is not for girls, especially the

152

well-brought-up ones who can recite the *'Rhodd Mam'* and never miss Sunday School and the Band of Hope. It has a zinc roof and stinks of boys. They are there every Saturday afternoon, pretending to be cowboys and Indians, shouting, whistling and thumping their feet when the film breaks down. The Forum is for the better class of person who comes to watch and to listen, although the matinee can be a pain at times with all the screaming and shrieking, for most well-brought-up girls are easily frightened.

I'll have to wait another year before I'm allowed to go to the first house on Saturday evenings. That's why I was so surprised when Mam said the three of us would be going to the Forum next Saturday.

'I don't mind,' I said, but I did mind, for girls of my age do not go to the pictures with their parents.

When I told her I'd rather go with Ann if that was all right with them, for they wouldn't enjoy it and Dad would probably fall asleep half way through the film, she said it was a play and not a film and if what she had read in the paper was true we had a treat in store.

It was true. These were not pictures on a screen but real people. When they laughed, we laughed with them; when they cried, we cried. We breathed the same air, shared their joy and their sadness, and when it was all over and we walked out into the darkness I felt as if I'd lost something and would never find it again.

Sunday morning, Mam, who had a far-away look

in her eyes, reminding me of Aunt Kate when she has one of her not-with-you days, said,

'Why can't we do something like that?'

'Like what?' Dad asked, blowing on his porridge.

'The play we saw last night.'

'We couldn't.'

'Why not?'

'Those people are professionals.'

We had to get our own meals for the next two days and eat them on our laps. Mam needed the table to hold the books she had borrowed from the library and the time to give them her whole attention, for there were so many things to consider when choosing a play.

By the time Dad came home on Wednesday, the choice and the tea had been made and all the books returned, except the chosen one.

'You've finished then,' he said, relieved that things were back to normal, for his knees are not made to hold plates.

'Finished?' Mam exclaimed. 'What about the cast, costumes, make-up, lighting, prompters, stage hands?'

'Do you need all those?' Dad asked.

'Of course we do. We may not be professionals, but a thing must be done properly, or not at all.'

It could have been 'not at all' and it would have been, too, if my father, the squire, hadn't said after another sleepless night of tossing and turning that the play should be cancelled. There have been reproaches and quarrels and falling out. Mrs Wyn-Rowlands, who's to be Lady Vaughan, the squire's wife, threatened to resign before she had even started because it was I who had been given the part of the maid, and not Llinos Wyn, and she accused my mother of keeping it in the family. Mam said she couldn't risk casting a ten year-old still in primary school in what was meant to be serious drama. The Reverend objected to playing a vicar and insisted on being a minister of religion. Mr Price, Chapel House, was very upset when Mam said he was too old to be the squire's son and only agreed to help when he was appointed stage manager. My mother had to warn Huw John, Robert and David John's father, the prodigal son who spends his days smoking and drinking rather than eating pig's swill, that there was to be no swearing, for this was Bethel Vestry, not the Queen's Arms.

All these troubles and loss of sleep have affected my father's concentration. Last night, he kept forgetting his lines and Mrs Wyn-Rowlands said he was supposed to be a member of the gentry, a pillar of society, and not a doddering old fool who couldn't even remember their son's name.

'He's no son of mine,' Dad muttered, which was one of the lines he'd forgotten.

When we got home, Mam told him she, as the producer, expected her husband to set a good example. That's when he said the play should be cancelled.

'How can you even suggest such a thing?' my

mother asked. 'After all the hard work I've put in, the abuse, the insults.'

'But is it worth it?'

'It will be. You give in far too easily, Richard. People throughout the ages have suffered for the sake of their art.'

*   *   *

The play got off to a bad start. My father's moustache wouldn't stay on and Make-up, who was Janet's mother, didn't know what to do. Mr Price, the stage manager, came to the rescue with a tube of glue, used to mend hymn books. The sisters had been at it for weeks searching the town for costumes and had worked night and day following the dress rehearsal, tucking in and letting out. No one had seen the Reverend since his dog collar had been taken off, to be washed and ironed. He was late arriving and came in through the back, having waited until everyone was inside. Costume couldn't get it back on and Mr Price came to the rescue once again with sticky tape, used to bind the hymn books after the glue had set.

'What would we do without our stage manager?' Mam said.

She had spoken too soon. We were ready on stage, Dad in his tweeds and bow tie, Mrs Wyn-Rowlands in a gown donated by the Francis sisters, and me all in black except for a little white apron and cap. But the curtain wouldn't open. Mr Price tugged at it and part of the set fell down. David John, one of the stage hands, ran to pick it up, telling the manager to move his foot as he was standing on the curtain. It flew open and the first thing the audience saw was David John's face peering through the plastic window.

'That scoundrel from the village is here again,' said Lady Vaughan. 'You must set the dogs on him, Charles.'

Squire Vaughan stood up, twirled his moustache, and said,

'Very well, my dear. Your wish is my command.'

As he crossed towards the door, Mam whispered from the wings,

'Keep to the script, keep to the script.'

The squire sat down again, I poured cold tea from a silver teapot into Madame Rees's best china, and the play began.

Make-up had done a very good job on Huw John. He looked like the devil himself. He only swore once, but that was enough to send Lady Vaughan into a fainting fit which the audience thought was part of the play but wasn't supposed to happen until the last act. The Reverend got stuck in the door and the whole set would have collapsed if the stage hands hadn't been there to hold it together. He helped himself to the biscuits, set out on a paper doily and only there for show, and spoke with his mouth full, which is something you should never do, especially on stage. Mr Pritchard, who used to be a member of the Home Guard, would have made a much better policeman than Sergeant Parry, who spends his days in the Station with the blind drawn and his feet up on the desk. Mam had told us not to stand there like statues, even if we had nothing to say, and I kept myself busy, fetching the smelling salts, dusting the furniture, and pouring tea back into the teapot for future use.

There was an interval before the last act so that the stage could be cleared, and Mr Price was sent to tell the audience to remain in their seats, for some of them thought the play had ended and were already on their way out.

When the curtain opened, Huw John, the squire's prodigal son, who had not been welcomed with open arms but thrown into a cell by Sergeant Pritchard, was on his knees, holding a Bible in one hand and looking up at the barred window. You could have heard a pin drop as he sang farewell to his mother and father, asking them to forgive him. It was the saddest song I had ever heard.

The curtain closed for the last time and the lights were switched on. We were clapped and cheered and my mother was presented with a bunch of flowers as an appreciation of all her hard work. As we took our bows, Dad sighed and whispered,

'Thank goodness that's over!'

We all had to wait for costume to attend to Lady Vaughan, for the Francis sisters were waiting to retrieve their gown. They stood there, rambling on about the old days and getting under everyone's feet. As Mrs Wyn-Rowlands, no longer Lady Vaughan, emerged from the little room behind the vestry, one of them said,

'What a difference clothes make!'

An exhausted Reverend had disappeared, anxious to get home before the sticky tape got unstuck, and Huw John had changed in the lavatory and left for the Queen's Arms with his make-up still on. Mr Pritchard was reluctant to change out of the policeman's uniform; he said that he had always wanted to join the police force but was refused because he was a few inches too short. I told him he would have made a much better policeman than Sergeant Parry. He smiled and lit his pipe. He only managed a few puffs before being sent out; for smoking, like swearing, is not allowed in Bethel Vestry.

My father, who thought everything was over, had forgotten about his moustache. Janet's mother didn't know how she was going to get it off and pulled at it with a finger and thumb asking all the time,

'Am I hurting you, Mr Owen?'

'Give it a quick pull,' Mam called, and away it came leaving my father with a patch of red, raw skin and tears in his eyes.

The set, which was falling apart by then, was soon taken down by the stage hands, with Mr Price giving the orders. Mrs Wyn-Rowlands, who still fancied herself as Lady Vaughan, told me to sweep up the crumbs the Reverend had spilt and to pack Madame Rees's china in tissue paper, to be returned to her on our way home. It was getting quite late by the time we had finished and I felt we had suffered more than enough for the sake of art.

We were having our supper and looking forward to a good night's sleep when Mam said,

'I was so proud of you, Richard. You didn't miss a single line.'

'And what about me?' I asked.

'A bit too free with the teapot perhaps, but you did very well.'

'There were quite a few hitches,' Dad said without moving his lips, still sore from the effects of the glue.

'Little hiccups, that's all. We learn from our mistakes. I think we should aim higher next time.'

'Shakespeare, perhaps?' Dad muttered.

Mam smiled and said, with the far-away look in her eyes,

'Why not? I'll call at the library first thing Monday morning.'

*   *   *

I'm sitting on the wall opposite the Catholic Church. I don't know how long I've been here, but it seems like hours. You can get piles from sitting on cold stone walls in the middle of winter, but I have more important things to worry about. That's why I'm here, waiting for Father Aidan to appear. I want to ask him if I can turn Catholic.

I should never have gone to that Christmas party in the Women's Institute. I wasn't supposed to be there, for Mam won't have anything to do with women who want to build Jerusalem in England's green and pleasant land rather than here, where they belong. I went because I felt sorry for Ann. The two with the highest marks in the end of term exams were to be moved up from 1B to 1A, but she only came tenth – although her eyes were no longer pink but red from studying by the light of a torch under the bedclothes. I couldn't understand why she wanted to go to the party, to be ignored by Megan and Elsie, but she said she had to show them that she didn't care, which she does. She bathed her eyes with boracic powder and persuaded Mrs Pugh to give her a home perm, which upset her routine for days.

I felt as Eleanor should have felt when she barged into our Christmas party, and even worse than when I sat alone at the little table in Elsie's house. I could hear Ann asking Megan Williams, 'Do you like it?' and Megan saying that it suited her, which wasn't true, but I suppose she could afford to be kind for once.

She insisted on sitting with Megan and Elsie and talked non-stop in a high-pitched voice. I couldn't take my eyes off her hair, still in tight little curls. She was afraid the perm would be ruined if she brushed it and she had sprayed it with hair lacquer. Even if I had been hungry, the smell would have put me right off my food. But the worst was still to come.

Last night, I tried to tell God what had happened, but I couldn't. Laziness, lying, disobedience, even insolence, are nothing compared to what I did with Billy Jones. I had never played Postman's Knock and I will never play it again as long as I live. One minute, I was there with all the others, not even pretending to enjoy myself; the next minute I was out in the porch with catch-a-fly Billy.

'What are we supposed to do now?' I asked.

'Close your eyes.'

I closed my eyes, thinking this was part of the game. Then I felt those big, blubbery lips pressing on mine. But instead of pulling back, as any decent girl would have done, I let him push his tongue into my mouth. It was soft and warm and tasted of blancmange and butter icing.

We must have been there some time, for when we returned they all shouted and clapped their hands.

'Did you do any French kissing?' Ann whispered.

'Tell you later,' I whispered back.

'Well, did you?' she asked again, as we were walking home.

'Did I what?'

'You know.'

I didn't know, but I wasn't going to let on.

'Yes, of course we did.'

'He put his tongue in your mouth!' she said, her little red eyes opening wide. 'Was it horrible?'

'It wasn't horrible at all. In fact, it was very nice.'

She stared at me for a moment, and then said, 'Oh, Helen!' in a Miss Hughes tone of voice. She was probably jealous, I thought, for there's a world of difference between knowing what French kissing means and doing it.

It wasn't until I was lying in bed that I realized what I had done. Even if I had managed to tell God, without going into too much detail, I knew there would be no forgiveness.

That's why I've been sitting here, waiting for Father Aidan to explain how to turn Catholic. It shouldn't be too difficult. If Mrs Wilson and her daughter managed it, then so can I. They used to be members of our chapel. Every Sunday evening, they would sit wherever the fancy took them, for Mrs Wilson didn't believe in paying to enter God's house. One Sunday, they had taken over our seat. It was before Dad became a deacon and my mother didn't want to spoil his chances by making a fuss. She did report it to the Reverend, however, and he promised to sort things out.

Off he went, like a lamb to the slaughter. I was sure Mrs Wilson would tell him that it was she who should be paid for listening to his sermons. But God was with him that day, as He should be. He's supposed to look after his servants, after all. Mrs W. had seen him coming, and when he reached the house, puffing and panting from climbing the hill, there was a note pinned to the front door with the two words 'Gone Catholic' written on it.

I don't know much about Catholics, but I read in *The Children's Guide to Knowledge* that they go into this box that looks like a telephone kiosk and tell the Father who's sitting behind bars that they have sinned. He'll want to know what it is, but it doesn't seem to matter for he always tells them they are forgiven. All they've got to do is to say a few 'Hail Marys' and that's it, until the next time.

I can see him walking towards me. He's young and handsome and I wonder if he knows what French kissing is. How did Ann know? I didn't. Christ forgave the people who crucified him because they didn't know what they were doing. Kissing Billy Jones was a very silly thing to do, but it wasn't a sin. At least, I don't think it was.

He smiles at me.

'Isn't it a bit cold to be sitting there?' he says, and walks on towards the church.

I stand up. My feet feel very heavy and as I walk I sway from side to side like Hannah-praise-the-Lord. It has all been a waste of time. With a father who is a deacon and a mother who is the Sunday School supervisor, I can never turn Catholic.

When I get home, Mam asks,

'Where on earth have you been?'

'Just for a walk.'

What would she say if I told her I had thought of going Catholic like Mrs Wilson, and how I'd like to sit in one of those telephone boxes with Father Aidan and tell him of my sin, which is not really a sin, just so that I could hear him say, 'You are forgiven, my child', his voice as warm as his smile. Tonight, instead of praying, I will say a few 'Hail

164

Marys full of grace' and imagine what it would be like to be kissed by him.

* * *

Ann and I have been home for our dinners. I would prefer to stay with the others, but Mam said it's cheaper for me to eat at home. Ann, of course, won't go near the canteen and complains that even the *smell* coming from there makes her feel sick. She's in one of her bad moods. Perhaps Porky Pugh had scoffed her dinner before she arrived. She'd be better off in the canteen in spite of the smell. I should have learnt to ignore these moods by now but she is, after all, my best friend and a greedy little brother is enough of a cross to bear without having to face Miss Evans on an empty stomach.

'Would you like an apple?' I ask.

I have one in my pocket, to eat during afternoon break, for Mam believes that an apple a day keeps the doctor away. Ann shakes her head. That's it, then. I've done my good deed for the day.

We are nearing the school gates when I hear her saying something. She's left it too late, for I've seen David John beckoning from behind the railings. He's been waiting for me while I was wasting my time and sympathy. When I tell Ann that I'll see her later, although I don't care if I won't, she grabs my arm and says,

'Why didn't you tell me?'

'Tell you what?'

'That your father was going to marry Miss Hughes Standard Four.'

'He wasn't.'

'Yes, he was. Eleanor told me. Her Nan said he dumped her.'

David John is still beckoning. The bell will be ringing soon. I push Ann away saying,

'Mind your own business.'

'I'd be ashamed if my father did something like that,' she says in a prim little voice.

I've never been able to forgive Miss Hughes or forget the 'we all know why, don't we' but I feel it my duty to defend my father although he was prepared to let me suffer so that Mam would not be hurt. I tell Ann he has nothing to be ashamed of and that it was Miss Hughes who wanted to marry him and would not leave him alone.

'Do you remember how she used to pick on me?' I ask.

'That was because you were cheeky.'

'Insolent.'

'Yes, that as well.'

'No it wasn't. It was revenge.'

'For what?'

When I tell her she's the most stupid person I know, she starts to snivel. Just then, Eleanor strides up to us, her tunic straining across her bosom. Barbara and Betty told me that after she returned home to her Nan she had to stay indoors during the

166

day and was only allowed out at night. But it's rather difficult to hide someone as large and as loud as Eleanor, and the school attendance officer found out. Her Nan agreed to let her go to school, for they both knew by then that her mother had decided not to let Eleanor cramp her style any longer. She's now in the B form with Ann and looks just the same although she was kept in the dark for so long.

'What has she been saying to you?' she asks Ann.

Ann whispers that she wouldn't dare repeat what I said. That's because it's true, but Eleanor glares at me saying I'd better wash out my mouth with soap and water. My once-best-friend tells Eleanor how I said she and her mother could go to 'h' 'e' double 'l' and that I had let Billy Jones put his tongue in my mouth. Eleanor Parry, who was caught doing disgusting things with catch-a-fly Billy behind Dwyryd Terrace, calls me a dirty little girl, links arms with Ann and says,

'Never mind her, you can be my friend.'

I'm late getting back to class, which means a black mark on my report. When I try to catch David John's eye, he turns his head away. He probably won't wait for me ever again, thinking I prefer being with tell-tale Ann, the most stupid person on earth.

The first lesson is Scripture with Miss Evans. We are told to write down in our books, 'To err is human, to forgive divine'.

'Do you know what that means?' she asks.

Megan Williams's hand shoots up.

'That God wants us to forgive those who sin against us, Miss.'

And Miss Evans, who has never forgiven anyone for sinning against her, smiles and says,

'And what should you do when you have sinned?'

My hand is now up, but instead of answering the question I ask if I may be excused. Miss Evans is disappointed. She probably hoped I would get it wrong so that she could have the pleasure of correcting me. As I leave the room I can hear Megan saying, 'Confess to God and ask his forgiveness', which is something she never has to do.

I stay in the lavatory for the rest of the lesson. If Miss Evans questions me I'll tell her I had stomach ache, which is quite true. The only comfort I have is knowing that Ann, too, will suffer for her sins, for having Eleanor Parry as a friend is the worst punishment I can think of. But even that isn't enough to keep me from shivering. Perhaps I should write a verse to pass the time and forget my troubles. Will it be about Ann who has betrayed me, or about Miss Evans who has never practised what she preaches? It's going to be that little red-eyed sneak, Ann Pugh.

When I get up off the seat, with a frozen bottom and chattering teeth, I've finished the verse:

> It's no good Ann saying sorry
> to God for being so sneaky

for she's now, I can tell,
on the wide road to hell
arm in arm with Eleanor Parry.

*   *   *

I've been kept in after school in what they call detention. The others, two girls and three boys, have all been here before and they know what to expect, but I don't. Miss Evans walks in, flapping her wings. If I'm to be punished, I'd rather it was anyone else except her. She sits at the high desk and asks us in turn why we are here. The fat girl next to me, who is in Form Three, is to write, 'I must not be insolent in class' a hundred times. Miss Evans eyes the girl's bosom, which reminds me of Eleanor's, and says in a sharp voice,

'Take that grin off your face, girl.'

She does try, but it seems to be stuck there. Two of the boys have been fighting in the school yard. They kick one another under the desk as they start on the 'I must not'. One of them is using two pencils, which means he can manage to write two lines at the same time.

They are all scribbling away before Miss Evans comes to me.

'And why are you here, Helen Owen?' she asks.

When I tell her it's because I forgot to do my homework, she repeats the question, and I mumble the same answer. She gives me a look that could kill and says,

'You are here because you lied, Helen Owen.'

The others raise their heads, and even the fat girl's grin disappears for a second. To be called a liar is much worse that being called insolent, which I thought was the worst sin of all.

I had meant to do my French homework after the Band of Hope, but David John asked me if I'd like to come for a walk. I refused to go down to the woods, which is only for courting couples, and nice girls who have just been to chapel do not go into dark places with boys. We walked around the town instead, touching, but not holding, hands, and he asked me if I would be his girlfriend. When I promised to think about it, he kissed me on the cheek, which was much nicer than what Ann called French kissing and nothing to worry about. I kept my promise, but forgot all about the homework.

Miss Thomas, who probably knows what French kissing is, having lived in France for two years, starts every lesson by saying '*Bonjour, mes enfants*' and we have to reply, '*Bonjour, Mademoiselle*'. I've tried to speak through my nose as she does, but it doesn't sound the same.

Today, when she asked if we had all done our homework, everyone, including me, answered,

'*Oui, Mademoiselle.*'

We had been told to write about ourselves. Miss Thomas began, of course, with Megan Williams, who can always be relied upon to set the standard. She had written a whole paragraph. Most of it was Double-Dutch to me, but when she had finished

Miss Thomas cried '*Très bien*', and waved her arms in the air.

There were only a few minutes left when she came to me. I started off quite well,

'*Je m'appelle Helen Owen. J'ai onze ans.*'

And that's all I could manage. It was when Miss Thomas asked, in English, for she knew her French would be wasted on me, why I had neglected to do my homework, that I said,

'I was absent, Miss.'

I should have known that the first thing she'd do was check the register which Mr Mathews fills in morning and afternoon, calling out our names in a tired voice and sighing between every tick.

'And is your name Helen Owen?' she asked.

'*Oui, Mademoiselle.*'

Some of the boys sniggered, for my 'oui' sounded like the word that rhymes with 'pee' and means the same.

So that's why I'm here in detention and having to write a hundred times, 'Honesty is the best policy'.

If I had been honest I would be here anyway, but forgetting to do my homework would not be regarded as a sin. The fat girl will tell Barbara and Betty, who are in the same form, and they will go around telling everyone else. From now on I'll be known not as the girl who was all tunic and no legs, which I managed to avoid, but as a liar, and no one will believe a word I say.

So that I'll have an excuse for being late, I decide to go to Nain's house, but I won't go near the room where it's always night. Uncle Jack is sitting by the fire with his eyes closed and Aunt Kate is standing facing the window, biting her nails. She says 'Hello', but I'm not quite sure yet if this is one of her with-you-days.

Uncle Jack takes some time to open his eyes and return from wherever he was.

'Have you settled down in your new school?' he asks.

'No, and I don't think I ever will.'

'You'll get used to it. It's something we all have to do.'

Aunt Kate stops her biting and turns to us, a worried look on her face, and asks,

'Get used to what?'

'Never you mind, Kate. Helen knows what I'm talking about, don't you?'

'I think I do. I'm there to stay, aren't I, and I have to make the best of it.'

'That's the only thing we can do,' says Aunt Kate.

Uncle Jack smiles at her.

'That's exactly what I said.'

'Is it? That's all right, then.'

The worried look disappears and she goes back to biting her nails.

*　　*　　*

I'd been trying to avoid Barbara and Betty, but when I arrived at chapel last night they were sitting on the wall, huddled together, so that all I could see was one body with two heads. I remembered the time I went to the fair with Mam and Dad and saw a notice outside a booth inviting people to come and see the two-headed woman. Mam had refused to let me go in, saying that it would give me nightmares.

I decided to wait by the gate until the others arrived, for there's safety in numbers, but I heard one of them calling,

'Why are you hiding from us, Helen Owen?'

'I'm not,' I said, for waiting under a street lamp can't be called hiding.

They had been told by the fat girl who couldn't take the grin off her face why I was kept in detention. I stood there, determined not to cry whatever names they called me, but one of them said what Miss Evans had called a lie was only an excuse and a very silly one.

'Was that the best you could do?' asked the other one.

'I didn't know what to say.'

'Shall we give her a few tips, Betty?'

'Only if she promises to ask her Mam if we can be in the drama next time.'

'I will. It's going to be Shakespeare.'

'We did him in English, didn't we, Barbara?' Betty said, adding in a very loud voice, 'To be or not to be, that is the problem.'

The Reverend had arrived. He leaned against the wall to regain his breath before saying that he, too, was an admirer of the Bard of Avon but that it should be 'that is the question'.

As I walk home with David John, I decide for now to leave the question whether Barbara and Betty can be or not be. Instead of telling us about God and Jesus, the Reverend spent the whole Band of Hope praising this Shakespeare until we were all sick and tired of hearing about him. He asked us questions no one could answer except little Janet-don't-know who said that someone called Romeo had poisoned himself because he thought Juliet, his girlfriend, was dead, which she wasn't. But when Juliet saw what he had done she, too, killed herself. Robert John thought it was a stupid thing to do and Llinos Wyn said that if he died everyone would say good riddance to bad rubbish.

'Would you kill yourself if I died?' David John asks as we cross the main street.

'No, I wouldn't, but I'd feel very sad.'

'And me.'

He knows now I'd rather be with him and that Eleanor Parry called me a dirty little girl for wishing Ann and her mother in hell, but I didn't tell him how I let Billy-catch-a-fly kiss me in the Women's Institute, for some things are best kept secret.

We say our good-byes and see-you-tomorrows and I walk on past Mrs Smith's house, taking care to keep to the other side. Mam will ask, as she always does, what we did in the Band of Hope tonight and I'll have to be careful not to mention Shakespeare, or Dad and I will be back to eating on our laps, and my promise to Barbara and Betty will have to be kept.

Dad has gone to visit Nain. They will talk about the old days when Dad and his brothers – Uncle Bob, who will never be killed by kindness, and Uncle John, who went to America to make his fortune and came home in a coffin – were boys, and Aunt Kate knew where she was and believed that she could be the future Edith Wynne. Instead of laughing as he does when he tells me of the fun they had and the tricks they played, Dad will sigh, for it was a long time ago and there is no happiness left in that room where it is always night. He will bring the sadness home with him and Mam, feeling the draught, will put some more coal on the fire and wait in silence until he becomes himself once again.

One night, when we were waiting for Dad to come home, she told me that she dreaded these Tuesday visits and would like to tell him what she thought of his mother, who was determined to make him feel miserable because he had gone against her wishes. But she had to hold her tongue, for men like my father, who are still little boys at heart, love their mothers and are blind to all their faults.

That's probably why she's sitting staring into the flames, thinking what she would-say-if-only. But it's not, for the first thing she asks is,

'What have you done to upset Ann?'

175

'I haven't done anything.'

'Mrs Pugh called tonight. She said Ann is in a terrible state.'

'That isn't my fault.'

'Her mother seems to think it is.'

Mrs Pugh had made sure I wasn't here to defend myself. But I won't be blamed for something I haven't done when there are so many things I have to be sorry for. I tell Mam what happened without explaining why I called Ann stupid and agree that it wasn't a nice thing to say, but if the cap fits . . . When I ask her how she would feel if she saw her best friend walking off arm in arm with Eleanor Parry, Mam says,

'Oh dear, it's no wonder poor Mrs Pugh was so upset.'

'And what about me?'

'You must do something about it, Helen.'

'Why should I?'

Mam ignores my question and sits staring into the flames once again. But she won't be thinking what she would-say-if-only tonight, for once she has decided something must be done it will.

That's why I've called at Ann's house on my way from school. Mam told me when we were having breakfast that it's for my own sake as much as Ann's, for wouldn't I prefer to be like Miss Jones Number Three rather than her next door?

'To err is human, to forgive divine,' I mumbled, between mouthfuls of corn flakes.

'Where did you learn those words . . . in Sunday School?' Mam asked, for my knowledge of the Bible makes her feel very proud.

'No, from Miss Evans in Scripture. It's like saying we are supposed to forgive those who sin against us.'

Mam frowned and said,

'I know what it means, Helen, but she certainly doesn't.'

Mrs Pugh opens the door. Even before she says, 'I'm so glad to see you, Helen', I know that her routine has been very seriously disturbed, for she isn't wearing her flowered cross-over apron. She shows me into the parlour, where Ann is lying on the settee with only the top of her head showing above a patchwork quilt.

I'm not going to ask her how she is, for I don't care. She mumbles something. It sounded like 'I'm sorry' but if she's going to apologize she'll have to do better than that.

'What did you say?'

'That I'm sorry. It's been terrible, Helen.'

'What has?'

'Being Eleanor Parry's friend.'

Her little eyes, which are now red from crying, peer at me over the edge of the quilt as she tells me how Eleanor bullied and threatened her and got her into trouble in class. She would barge into their house and eat all the food, shouting and swearing and saying dirty things.

'Like what?' I ask.

'You know.'

'No, I don't.'

'It's better that you don't.'

There have been no clean clothes for a fortnight and no Victoria Sandwich and no bike on her birthday, for the order has been cancelled.

'Will you be my friend again?' she asks in a very pathetic little voice.

'I suppose so.'

'I'm glad Miss Hughes didn't marry your father.'

She's got it right this time, at least.

'So am I. Do you want me to call for you tomorrow morning?'

'Yes, please. What will I do with Eleanor?'

'Dump her. Send her to Coventry. Tell her she can go to hell on her own now that your best friend is back.'

Ann throws the quilt off. I hope she's not going to give me a hug, because I'm not ready for that yet, but she only smiles and says,

'I'll never be nasty to you again.'

As I leave the house, I can hear her telling her mother that everything's going to be all right now and please may they have Victoria Sandwich tomorrow although it's Thursday.

* * *

'Is the pain any better now, Helen?'

My mother's concern frightens me. She must think I'm really ill, for I heard her whispering to my father that she should have told me but had hoped it wouldn't happen for some time yet. He, too, is acting strangely, as if he's afraid to look at me. What is it she should have told me? I need to know, but I'm too afraid to ask.

When my father suggests they should send for Doctor Jones, my mother says he should know there's no need for that and will he stay with me for she's got some shopping to do.

'Have you got to go now?' he asks.

She nods and Dad says,

'Don't be long. There's a choir practice at half past five.'

He doesn't want to stay with me. It isn't because he thinks choir practice is more important than a sick daughter. Never having been ill himself, he can't cope with any kind of illness or sadness. I remember how upset he was when Mam told him Mr Jenkins the Co-op had died and that he should call to see Mrs Jenkins before any one else stepped in. Dad protested he couldn't possibly do that, and what would she think of him discussing gravestones when she had just lost her husband?

'She wouldn't need your services if he was still alive,' Mam said. 'Like it or not, you make your living out of the dead.'

'I don't like it,' Dad said and, realizing that she'd gone too far, Mam left it at that.

If it wasn't for my mother he wouldn't have a living at all. She's the one who makes sure the bills are settled, for he doesn't have the heart to demand money from grieving widows.

'I thought you'd done your shopping this morning,' Dad says.

Mam doesn't answer. That would mean telling a lie, for I know where she's going.

'I'll be as quick as I can.'

She's gone, and my father is sitting at the table with his back towards me. It could be hours before Mam returns. Doctor Jones won't make any house calls until he's finished surgery, unless it's an emergency. But perhaps this *is* an emergency and Miss Edwards, who knows more about us than we do ourselves, will shout through the hole in the wall that the Doctor has been called out and they have the choice of waiting or going home and taking a couple of aspirins. Most of them will choose to stay rather than confess there's nothing wrong with them. They wouldn't be there if Doctor Richards was on duty, but Doctor Jones will never send anyone away without a prescription, which will make them feel better even if they don't need it.

They'll be queuing out in the street tonight, for Doctor Richards doesn't believe in working on a Saturday. If you want to see him, and not many do, you'll have to suffer until Monday. I wonder if Mam will push her way through and knock on the little door in the wall which Miss Edwards keeps closed between her and all the germs? Although the surgery must be the unhealthiest place in town, Miss Edwards is never ill. Mam says she's immune to it all, which probably means she takes care not to breathe in when she has to open the door.

It's so quiet here that I can hear Miss Evans moving around next door. How will she feel if Doctor Jones has to send for an ambulance to take me to hospital? Will her guilty conscience keep her awake at night? The pain is getting worse and I can't bear the silence any longer.

'What's wrong with me, Dad?' I ask.

'You'd better ask your mother.'

'But I want to know now. Am I very ill?'

'You're growing up, that's all. Mam will explain.'

I won't need an explanation, for I've just thought of that day under the bridge when Eleanor pulled down her knickers and Ann said it happened to everyone except boys. Ann's mother had told her it didn't hurt, but it does.

'It'll soon pass,' Dad says.

Isn't that what he always says when things go wrong? My father thinks every cloud has a silver lining. When he sings about the girl who had been turned away from her home, the door is never locked. I understand now why my grandmother said, 'That's what he wants to believe'. But as my mother once said, living with an optimist can be very hard at times. I looked the word up and it means one who sees the best in everything. I suppose being a man helps, for he doesn't have to face this terrible pain. Growing up means suffering like this once a month, having breasts and wearing a brassiere so that they don't flop around, and crouching over the lavatory

181

seat rather than sitting on it. The only thing I have to be thankful for is that this hadn't happened when I let Billy Jones put his tongue in my mouth.

As soon as Mam returns, Dad hurries off to his choir practice humming one of the hymns. Mam waits until he's well out of sight and hearing before handing me a parcel wrapped in brown paper.

'Do you understand what's happening, Helen?' she asks.

I nod and say,

'I could have a baby now if I wanted to.'

'Who told you that?'

'I can't remember. It doesn't matter anyway. The last thing I want is a stinking baby like horrible Bobby.'

I expect her to tell me that the 's' word is one that nice girls never use but she only smiles and says,

'Perhaps you'll change your mind one day when you are married, with a good man like your father to take care of you.'

When I tell her I don't want to marry anyone, and that I'm going to stay at home with them so that Dad can take care of us both, Mam puts her arms around me. I snuggle up to her. Her body is as soft and comforting as a hot water bottle. The pain is still there but, as my father said, it will soon pass. I think maybe I should make an effort to see at least the good, if not the best, in everything and everyone, but as I realize this pain will have to be suffered once a month for ever more I know that, however hard I try, I can never be an optimist or another Auntie Lizzie.

*　　*　　*

'Tell it again, Dad. Just once more.'

The girl, who is still a child here in this room where she is warm and safe, laughs, as she always does. With the curtains closed between her and the cold dark night, all's well with the world.

She goes upstairs, with no sad thoughts to make her shiver. The warm nest is waiting for her. She snuggles into it, closes her eyes, and asks God to:

Remember me and Mam and Dad,
Aunt Kate, who doesn't know where she is
and Uncle Jack, who'd rather be somewhere else,
Amen.